BALLET
STORIES

D1147615

With many thanks to Donald and John for all their help.

KINGFISHER
An imprint of Kingfisher Publications Plc
New Penderel House, 283-288 High Holborn
London WC1V 7HZ
www.kingfisherpub.com

First published by Kingfisher 1997
2 4 6 8 10 9 7 5 3 1

A CIP catalogue record for this book is available from the British Library.

ISBN 0 7534 1013 3

Printed in India

1TR/0204/THOM/MA/90HIB/F

1TS/0904/THOM/MA/90HIB/F

BALLET
STORIES

CHOSEN BY
HARRIET CASTOR

ILLUSTRATED BY
SALLY HOLMES

KINGFISHER

CONTENTS

SAMANTHA AND LIZINKA

SUSAN CLEMENT FARRAR

from Samantha on Stage

A Russian girl, Lizinka, has joined Samantha's ballet class. Now that the school is about to mount a production of "The Nutcracker", Samantha wonders who will win the part of Clara, the little girl at the centre of the ballet's story.

"**W**ELCOME BACK, CLASS," said Miss Jan with a smile. "Now that the holidays are over, I hope you are all ready to settle down to some real hard work." There was a tenseness in the air, a realization that today they would be assigned their special parts in *The Nutcracker*.

"Class will break five minutes early," Miss Jan continued, "so that I can tell you more about our recital plans. Right now, let's get to the *barre* and try to pull ourselves back into shape. I'm sure we've all indulged in too much good food and lazy habits."

Smiling sheepishly and nodding in agreement, the class assembled at the *barre* and started their *pliés*. As they progressed from one exercise to another, here and there a muffled groan could be heard when an exercise put demands on their muscles.

Samantha felt a happy tingle as she bent and stretched with

all her might, trying to push all thoughts of the recital out of her mind. She had taken special care to pull her hair up in a knot off her neck. But as she exercised, a few short tendrils escaped from her upswept hair and hung in springy little wisps around her face. It was nice to be dancing again. She felt a kinship to all the people in this classroom who shared the love of dance with her. Glancing at Lizinka, she felt a common bond that even the width of an ocean could not separate.

So absorbed was she in her own thoughts that she was startled to hear Miss Jan's voice call out, "Centre floor, please, class. Take a partner; dancers to right face upstage, and dancers to left face downstage." Before Samantha could collect her thoughts, she found Lizinka beside her, a tentative smile on her face. Her solemn blue eyes questioned Samantha.

"Be my partner, Sam?" Lizinka asked softly. Looking back with a slight toss of her head, Sam nodded lightly. Observing Sam, one would never guess she was almost bursting with pride.

Positioning themselves on the floor, they waited for instructions from their teacher. There was some scuffling and giggling over choosing partners. Miss Jan waited patiently; then she said:

"Starting with the right foot and working back to back with your partner, do *balancé, balancé soutenu,* turn, three times. All will finish to front on third turn. *Arabesque* right; step left, and *tendu* right back. Then *port de bras.* Let's all mark it before trying it to music."

Samantha looked at Lizinka, eyebrows raised. She thought she understood the combination, but for some unknown reason she held back. Usually Sam plunged into her dance steps with great confidence, but Lizinka's presence made her reluctant to do it, for fear of making a mistake. Glancing at Lizinka, she could sense her assurance, and with it her own confidence returned.

"And a . . . *balancé, balancé soutenu*, turn, and one two three, one two three, one two three four five six. *Balancé, balancé soutenu*, turn, to the front. *Arabesque* two three, step two three. *Port de bras* two three four five six."

There was a little fumbling here and there, and questions about positioning of arms by some, and then a quieting down and feeling of readiness to try again.

"And . . . a . . . *balancé, balancé soutenu*, turn." Miss Jan continued on through the combination again. This time it went more smoothly and picked up speed. Another time through and they were ready for the music.

Sam's eyes shone as she listened to the delightful waltz melody. It sounded familiar to her, yet she couldn't actually name it.

"You are dancing to the music from *The Nutcracker*," Miss Jan explained. "Isn't it beautiful? It's the *Waltz of the Flowers* – are we ready to try our combination to it?"

Going to the record player, she started the music again, counting through the introduction, leading them into the steps.

Samantha lost herself in the movement of the dance, enjoying it so completely that she felt a twinge of sadness when it was over. She was pulled back to reality when Miss Jan said, "Very good, class. Now please sit down so I can talk to you about your recital parts."

A hush came over the studio. As Samantha sat down, she again found herself next to Lizinka. She was afraid the class could hear her heart pounding in her breast.

"I've given a great deal of thought to casting in this ballet, because of course we want it to be very good. First of all, let me say that all of you, except the one who plays the part of Clara, will be dancing to the *Waltz of the Flowers*. You have been doing so well on toe – or to be correct, I should say *en pointe*," she said smiling, "that you have just learned one of the combinations in your recital dance in class today!"

"Really? That was fun. What do we wear?" Words tumbled over one another in the girls' excitement.

"Each one of you will be able to choose your favourite colour," their teacher said. "Your costume will be a classic *tutu*, and you'll wear a garland of flowers in your hair. It will be very elegant." Miss Jan paused, looking first at one and then another.

"However, it means a lot of hard work, as you must dance with a teenage girl who will be playing the Queen of the Flowers. You are her *corps de ballet*. Do you think you can handle it?" Miss Jan asked this seriously.

Their sparkling eyes made it clear that they were very pleased.

"Now," Miss Jan continued, taking a deep breath, "I've had to cast four of you in the first act as guests of the Governor and his wife – the little cousins who come to the Christmas party with their parents, remember? I couldn't choose all of you, as it would overcrowd the stage. Since I'd like an even number of boys and girl, and since the boys in the dance class are not too tall, I decided to choose the shortest girls in this class for the young guests. Any one of you would be capable of playing the part, as it calls for more acting then dancing."

"Who is Clara?" they burst out almost in unison. "You said she'd be from this class!"

"So I did, so I did!" She laughed. "I thought I'd wait to tell you that news last, but since you all are so impatient, I won't keep you in suspense any longer. It was a very difficult decision, and I thought long and hard before making a choice . . ."

Samantha closed her eyes for an instant and said a little prayer.

Her hands were clasped tightly in her lap. Opening her

eyes, she could see Miss Jan talking, but the voice seemed to drone on and on from a great distance. The words had no meaning. She leaned forward and held her breath to stop the pounding in her head, just as the words "Lizinka for the part of Clara" reached her ears.

She heard the class react with excitement and she saw the look of pure joy come over Lizinka's face. Samantha's face felt like a mask. She blinked fast to keep the tears back and felt her lips stretch into a stiff little smile.

"Debby, Michelle, Naomi, and Samantha will be the little cousins," Miss Jan finished, then said, "Ready for your *révérence*, class." Everyone stood to get into place for her final bow. Samantha took this time to regain her composure and hide her disappointment.

As the class ended, some of the girls gathered around Lizinka, congratulating her. Some talked about their *Waltz of the Flowers*, others about their parts as young guests.

Only alert Naomi sensed Sam's misery. "You should have the lead, Sam," she whispered in her ear as she squeezed Sam hard around the neck.

Trying to keep the disappointment out of her face, Sam moved towards Lizinka. Her voice sounded shrill to her own ears, but she smiled brightly as she congratulated Lee on being picked for the part of Clara.

"I'm glad we're in Act One together," Lizinka said. Nodding quickly, Samantha gathered her clothes in a little bundle as if in a hurry and quickly stepped out of the studio.

Walking briskly towards home, she was thankful that it was a little dusky, for she could no longer hold back the tears that stung her eyes and rolled down her cheeks.

"I must be a good sport," she scolded herself. "Lizinka deserved the part."

As she rounded the corner to her home, a sob escaped. How could she tell her mother about this? She bit her lip hard to keep back the tears. Entering the kitchen, she saw her mother talking on the phone. Mrs Scott's smile of welcome changed to one of concern when she saw Sam's face.

11

"Are you all right, Sam, dear?" she asked with a worried look, holding her hand over the mouthpiece.

"I've got a little stomachache," Sam answered, holding her hand over her stomach and smiling weakly at her mother. "Think I'll just go to bed," she said, heading for her room.

She lay on her back. The pillow felt cool and smooth on her hot cheek, and the darkness enveloped her so that she felt safe from prying eyes. No need to hide her disappointment now. No need to pretend anymore. Not until she had wept long and hard and found herself completely drained of all emotion did she hear a gentle knock on her door.

"May I come in, Sam?" her mother asked, pushing the door open softly as she said it. She felt her mother's comforting arms around her. Her mother knew. There was no need for words. No need for explaining. She understood.

The winter months were cold and long, but for Samantha the days flew by. There was schoolwork, of course, but most of that was done in the classroom. Luckily Samantha's teacher felt that children should not be burdened with too much homework. Her friends took their skates to school and they all gathered on the Common for a few whirls after class. By four-thirty it was dark, so Samantha had to head for home. She liked to help her mother set the table, and she loved making the salad so much that it became her self-appointed chore. Then she put on her ballet record and faithfully went through her *barre* work. She had set herself the goal of improving her extension. Lizinka was able to raise her leg so high that it was the envy of all the class.

Ballet became more and more an important part of Sam's life, and observing Lizinka, she began to realize it was a jealous art, demanding dedication and hard work. With the young Prince in *The Nutcracker*, Lizinka had begun to practise her *pas de deux*, which in the language of ballet means "dance for two". Sam watched Lizinka bend and stretch her body to the fullest, stoically putting demands on it until beads of perspiration glistened on her forehead. She realized that she had never really worked very hard. In the past when she had become tired, she had quit. More and more now she made herself stretch her body until she became aware of each muscle and felt it tingle. She actually began to enjoy the feeling of being physically exhausted – looking forward to her hot bubble bath and cosy flannel nightgown after her one-and-a-half-hour exercise session.

As the weeks went by, she became aware of the appreciative glances of her ballet class when she extended her leg at the *barre*, stretched it high above her waist, and held it there. She accepted their appreciation gratefully, with a sense of satisfaction, knowing she had worked hard for their approval. It had become more than just a desire to outshine Lizinka. Now, because of her growing commitment to the beautiful art of ballet, Sam wanted to be the best for her own sake.

She haunted the studio, coming to class early and lingering after the others had gone home. One late afternoon her mother called, worried, and Miss Jan laughingly told her that Sam was still there, safe and sound. Miss Jan understood

Sam's love for dance, and would allow her to work quietly at the *barre* as long as she did not interfere with the practice of her regular classes.

Now and then Sam and Miss Jan would have little conversations about ballet, and Sam felt a bond with her teacher, who shared the same feelings about dance that she was beginning to develop.

The *Waltz of the Flowers* was a difficult but beautiful dance. Sam worked until she knew it perfectly. She even learned the Queen's part, and her toes became stronger as each day passed. She loved it all, but most of all she loved the dance that Lizinka, as Clara, did with the Prince. The dancer who took the part of the Prince was a handsome, blond boy about thirteen years old. Tom was tall, slim, and self-assured. When Lizinka came forward on her toes and extended her leg into an elegant *arabesque*, he would promenade around, turning her on the tip of her toe. It took Sam's breath away, it was so lovely. Then Lizinka would do two *piqué* turns and Tom would lift her high into the air, while her arms did a graceful *port de bras*, and her legs went into a *grand jeté*. Sam would watch as she continued to work quietly at the *barre*, determined that someday she would have her chance. When that time came, she would be prepared!

January, February, and March passed quickly by. Rehearsals began in earnest, and the girls started acting their parts. As one of the young guests, Samantha had to learn two German dances, which were lots of fun.

The march was done with the little "boy cousins", who were her own age. It was lively and gay; the boys teased, and the girls giggled, and that was the way Miss Jan liked it. It was a Christmas party, and they were supposed to be having fun.

The *Grandfather Dance* was done with the older teenage boys, who took the parts of the uncles. It was a German folk dance, and the boys picked up the girls and whirled them right off their feet. They were breathless when they finished, cheeks rosy and eyes sparkling with laughter.

In the middle of the dance Uncle Drosselmeyer, who was

very old and eccentric, wore a funny hat, and carried a crooked cane, pretended to be gruff and cross. The "cousins" had to make believe they were afraid of him.

Uncle Drosselmeyer came laden with gifts for the children. He gave Franz a drum, and Clara received a beautiful nutcracker made in the shape of a handsome soldier. This was the most exciting part of the ballet because Franz, who was jealous, grabbed it away from Clara and ran around and around, with the girls shrieking and the boys yelling. Franz's parents were so terribly embarrassed, they sent him to bed.

Samantha's part as a little cousin was over when the guests left, but she and the others all liked to watch Lizinka, as Clara, come back into the living room, cuddle in the big easy chair with her broken nutcracker, and pretend to fall asleep. Lizinka took it very seriously. When the Prince appeared from behind the Christmas tree and walked forward, arms outstretched to her, Samantha's friends all tittered and whispered. But Lizinka stayed in character. She solemnly reached her hand out and stood gracefully. The Prince then led her across the stage into the next scene, which was the Land of Snow.

When Lizinka and Tom did their *pas de deux*, Sam never left the studio until they had finished practising. They worked terribly hard and never complained of being tired. It was then that Samantha realized why Miss Jan had chosen Lizinka. If Sam had not been exposed to Lizinka's hard work, she would never have realized how much is expected of a lead. Watching Lizinka work, she knew Miss Jan had been right in her choice. Another year – another time – Sam would be ready. She understood the demands now. At first she had thought only of the pretty costume and the glory of the part, never realizing that this glory must be earned through hard and dedicated work.

In April their costumes arrived. They were breathtaking in their beauty. Each was a different colour – ballet-pink, sky-blue, sunshine-yellow, spring-green, pale orchid – all with classic *tutus* that stood straight out from the waist, making Sam aware of why they were taught to hold their arms rounded. It was to reach around the ballet skirts.

Samantha's costume was sky-blue and it was caught up with small clusters of pale pink roses. There was also a garland of pink rosebuds for her hair. She felt like a princess when she tried it on and put the flowers in her blond hair.

One day as they were rehearsing Act One, they came to the part where Uncle Drosselmeyer gave Clara the nutcracker, which made Franz jealous. He grabbed the nutcracker out of Clara's hands and ran around the living-room stage, followed by all the other little boy cousins. The girl cousins raced after them, and there was a tug of war; Franz and the boys pulled one way, and Clara and the girls pulled the other way until – kerplunk! down went the girls and—crash!—the nutcracker landed on the floor and was broken. Clara burst into tears and ran to the dancer who was playing her mother.

Just at that moment the studio door opened, and a woman came in. She walked over to Miss Jan and said something to her in a low voice.

Miss Jan immediately went to the tape recorder and turned it off.

Lizinka looked up quickly, expecting a correction of some kind to be forthcoming since Miss Jan often stopped the music to offer suggestions or make changes of some kind.

"Lizinka," Miss Jan said with a smile, "your mother is here to pick you up. You may be excused for the rest of the day."

Lizinka's face flushed when she saw her mother. She immediately left the studio floor and went over to her. Putting her arm around her daughter's shoulder, Mrs Petrovna said something to Lizinka that made her look sad.

Samantha couldn't help staring, concerned for her friend. Suddenly she became aware that everyone was looking at her.

"Put your toe shoes on," said Naomi. "Yes, go ahead."

"Hurry up," she heard her friends say.

Puzzled, she looked at Miss Jan.

"I don't think you heard me, Samantha. I asked you to take Lizinka's place for this rehearsal, please."

"Who, me?" stammered Samantha, feeling sure this was some sort of joke.

"Yes." Miss Jan laughed. "You. Will you hurry and put on your toe shoes and warm up for the *pas de deux* with Tom?"

"I-I-I can't do that!" Samantha said desperately.

"Why, I thought you would jump at the chance. Don't you want to?" her teacher asked, puzzled.

"Oh, I do, I do, but, but, but—"

The class broke into laughter.

"You sound like a motorboat," said Michelle, giggling.

"The rest of you may leave now, and I'll work with Samantha and Tom alone for a while. See you all on Thursday," said Miss Jan.

As if in a dream, Samantha went over and started to put on her toe shoes. Her hands were cold, and her whole body felt numb. Could it really be true? Was she to practise the *pas de deux* with the Prince? Her fingers were so stiff, she fumbled as she tied the ribbons of her toe shoes. Automatically she walked over to the *barre* to warm up, as she had seen Lizinka

17

do. Timidly she glanced over at Tom, who was preoccupied with a combination of steps he was trying to master.

"I'll never make it," Samantha said to herself. "They'll laugh at me." Frantically she continued working out until her body became more relaxed. She inhaled deeply, and her heart gradually stopped its wild pounding.

"I must keep calm. I must do my best," she reasoned sensibly to herself. "I *know* the dance. I've watched it enough. I've even practised it, but always alone, never with a partner."

"Ready, Samantha?" Miss Jan asked, and she turned on the recorder. "Just do the best you can, dear. Tom will help you."

Shakily Samantha walked toward Tom. He reached out and took her hand. His hand was strong and steady. She stood on one toe and raised her leg into a high *arabesque*. Thank goodness I've been practising at home, she thought. At least I can get my leg up above my waist. Not quite as high as Lee, but almost.

Slowly, Tom started to promenade around with her. How strange it seemed, but fun. Suddenly, when she was three quarters of the way around, she began to wobble on her toes. She lost her balance and down she went into a crumpled heap.

For a moment she thought she was going to cry. Then, looking up out of the corner of her eye, she could see Tom grinning down at her. She quickly glanced at Miss Jan, who was smiling, too. Why, they want to help me, she thought. They are not going to laugh at me 'cause I make mistakes. They're on my side, and I won't let them down. Jumping up quickly, she said in a quiet, steady voice, "I'm sorry. May I try that again? I think I can do it, with a little more practice."

"I'm sure you can, Samantha," said Miss Jan, and there was a look of pride on her face.

For over an hour they worked, quietly and steadily. Learning to hold their bodies erect and centred so as not to go off balance was not easy. But with repetition it became better, and by the end of the lesson it was a fairly presentable little *pas de deux*.

Miss Jan was pleased. Samantha could tell. And Tom seemed satisfied too.

"Lizinka's mother is going away for a month. She had to leave tonight. That is why she came for Lizinka," Miss Jan said. "There will be times when Lee won't be able to come to rehearsals, and I want Tom to continue his practice. On those occasions, Samantha," Miss Jan said seriously, "I'd like you to be Lizinka's understudy. That means when she is not here, I'd like you to practise in her place. Would you like that, Sam?"

"Would I? Wow! I'll say I would!" Samantha fairly shouted. Then, worried, she looked at Tom to see how he felt about it.

He was smiling and nodding his head. "Great," he said. "You make a fine understudy, and I do need the practice."

"I'll do my best," Samantha said solemnly, looking from one to the other, then quickly turned away as she felt the tears sting her eyes. What a day this has been, she thought. Do you suppose I'm dreaming?

"Mum! Mum!" shouted Samantha as she rushed into the kitchen. "Guess what?"

Samantha's brown eyes sparkled with joy. As usual, one blond braid on the top of her head had escaped the elastic band and was sticking straight out to one side, giving her a very impish look. Her flushed face was dead serious, however, and Mrs Scott knew this was a matter that would demand her entire attention.

"What is it, Samantha?" she asked anxiously.

"I'm an understudy! I'm an understudy," shouted Sam joyously.

Mrs Scott breathed a sigh of relief. Whatever it was all about, at least she could tell that it was good news.

"Simmer down!" she laughed. "What do you mean? Weren't you at ballet rehearsal today?"

"That's just it," Sam said eagerly. "I was at rehearsal, and Lizinka's mother came in to get her because she had to go away on a trip – her mother did, I mean – and Miss Jan asked me to take Lee's place."

Samantha stopped short, looking at her mother. Her brown eyes seemed to give off electric sparks. She had never been so excited.

"So you played the part of Clara in the first act?" her mother asked cautiously, still not quite sure.

"I mean, Mother," Samantha said, very slowly and distinctly, as if speaking to a small child who did not quite understand, "I mean, that I did the *pas de deux* with the Prince!"

"You did?" Mrs Scott said, unbelieving. "Really?"

Before the words had escaped her lips, Samantha, who had been sitting tensely on the edge of the chair, could no longer contain herself. Like a tight coil unwinding, she sprang across the room, and before either of them knew what had happened, Sam was in her mother's arms, laughing and crying at the same time. All the tensions of the past two hours were released, and now she felt completely exhausted.

They were chattering like a couple of magpies and didn't

notice Mr Scott standing at the kitchen door.

Coming forwards toward Samantha, he made a big awkward bow, saying, "Well, my little girl will be a famous ballerina yet!"

"Oh, Dad," – she giggled, – "stop teasing. Who told you about it anyway?" she asked suspiciously.

"Why, I've been standing here for five minutes." Mr Scott laughed. "Nobody noticed me, though. If this is what it's like to have a famous daughter, I'm not sure I'm going to like it."

"Oh, Dad, don't be silly. I'm only going to take Lee's place when she's not around, so Tom can keep up with his practice." She tried hard to be matter-of-fact about it all. But a grin played around her lips, and her sparkling eyes gave her away.

"Tell us about it , honey," Mrs Scott insisted.

While Mrs Scott made them some cocoa, Sam related in detail the events of the afternoon. She could even tell them about her tumble without feeling bad, knowing that she had made a lot of progress from that moment on.

"I think this calls for a celebration, don't you, Beth?" Mr Scott said, looking over at his wife questioningly.

Pleased that he would realize the importance of the situation, Mrs Scott smiled tenderly at her husband. The dinner she had started to prepare could be eaten tomorrow. This indeed was a special day for Sam. Remembering when her daughter had come home with a "stomachache," Mrs Scott could smile now at how things had worked out. She was proud that Samantha had made the best of the situation and had gone on rehearsing harder than ever. Sam had learned a lot from that bitter lesson. Disappointments made success that much sweeter.

"Get your hats, ladies. I'm taking my two best girls out to dinner," Mr Scott said gallantly.

"Hats?" they said, laughing. "What hats? Let's go!"

REHEARSAL REVENGE

JAHNNA N. MALCOLM

from Scrambled Legs: We Hate Ballet!

Rocky, Mary Bubnik, Gwen, McGee and Zan are five girls with one thing in common: they've all been forced to join Deerfield's Academy of Dancing – and they all hate ballet! Cast in the school's version of "The Nutcracker", they find themselves clashing with their snooty, ballet-mad classmates, nicknamed the Bunheads.

"**R**EMEMBER, KEEP your hands fluttering in front of your face," Miss Jo reminded the girls as she ran them through the steps for the mouse dance. "Like little Whiskers."

"That's the easy part," Mary Bubnik whispered to Gwen.

"And keep your *jetés* high and clean," Miss Jo called out.

"That's the hard part," Gwen grumbled as she struggled to keep up.

McGee did a couple of *jetés* in a circle, leaping as high as she could. "Don't forget," she said to Gwen, "you're an athlete. Strong and powerful."

"Right. I'm an athlete." Gwen threw herself into the next *jeté*. She landed with a thud and caught a glimpse of herself in the mirror with her stomach sticking out. "That's a laugh."

"No, no, Mary Bubnik," Miss Jo called out. "Turn to the left, not the right."

Mary Bubnik grinned, turned to the left and promptly ran into Zan, who was trying not to draw any attention to herself.

"Sorry," she apologised.

"It's all right," Zan whispered. "Stay in front of me, OK? It's almost over."

The girls ran in a ragged circle, then burst apart on Miss Jo's command. As they went into their final leaps, Rocky and McGee's grand *jetés* were extra high. Rocky even threw in a karate kick and yell.

Mrs Bruce hit one last resounding chord and Miss Jo clapped her hands. "That was a very good start. So much enthusiasm is nice to see!"

McGee gave Rocky a high five. Gwen and Mary Bubnik grinned at each other. Even Zan felt a little encouraged.

"Gather around me in a circle on the floor, girls," Miss Jo instructed. "Now that you know the steps to the dance—"

"Who said we know the steps?" Mary Bubnik asked, wide-eyed. She was having trouble remembering whether it was two *jetés* and a run, run, run, or three.

Miss Jo smiled and continued. "It is important to know the story of your part in the ballet. Then we can add the acting, which is as important to the performance of this dance as the steps."

"Oh, great," Gwen grumbled to Rocky. "First she tells me I have to dance. Now I have to act? If singing is included in all of this, you can count me out."

Rocky gave Gwen a swift jab in the side. "I like acting."

"So?" Gwen blinked at her. "I don't."

"Shhhh!" Zan put her finger to her lips. She knew the story by heart but she was eager to hear Miss Jo tell it.

"You all remember that Clara was given a magical nutcracker at the Christmas party?"

The five girls nodded.

"Well, after the party," Miss Jo began, "at the stroke of midnight a magic spell takes hold of the entire household." She lowered her voice dramatically. "That's when the Mouse King gathers his evil forces."

23

"That must be us!" Mary Bubnik sang out.

"That's right." Miss Jo leaned forward. "At first you are just a haunting whisper rustling in the shadows."

Outside, the sun went behind a cloud and the room darkened for a fraction of a second. Without thinking, Zan and Mary Bubnik shivered.

"Then the mice become a terrifying force, an army of the night," Miss Jo continued.

Rocky whispered, "I like that."

"From every corner of the old mansion, you come creeping and scurrying, getting ready for battle."

The girls leaned forward, hanging on Miss Jo's every word. Her voice fell to a whisper. "At first your movements are tiny. *Jeté, jeté*, and run, run, run." She demonstrated with her long hands.

"Then the Nutcracker appears, and you show your power." Miss Jo's voice grew stronger and the girls sat up straight. "Violent movements. *Grand jetés*. We want to scare the Nutcracker and his army, so our movements are ungraceful and grotesque. No pointed toes.

"That's a relief," Mary Bubnik said. "When I point my toes, these big old shoes of mine always flop off."

"And your expressions are frightening, like a creature from a nightmare," Miss Jo added. She made a face at them, and the girls all laughed.

"Geez, Louise," McGee chuckled, "this could be fun."

Zan kept quiet. It didn't sound like fun to her. The fact of the matter was, she would still have to get up in front of all those people and make a fool of herself.

"Now, let's try the dance again," Miss Jo announced. "Only this time, try to act your parts. Think like mice, *be* mice."

She was interrupted by a stirring at the door. The gang looked up to see Courtney and Page peeking around the corner, wide grins on their faces. Alice Westcott and a few of the other Bunheads were grouped behind them in the hall.

"Oh, great!" Gwen muttered to McGee. "You don't think they saw us rehearsing, do you?"

"I hope not," Zan whispered back. "We'll never hear the end of it."

"Come in, come in!" Miss Jo waved the girls into the room. "Mr Anton's group will be joining us for the final part of our rehearsal," she explained to the mice.

"Perfect," Gwen groaned. "Just perfect!"

Mr Anton stepped into the studio, followed by a tall, dark-haired boy with electric blue eyes. Gwen and Mary Bubnik gasped out loud.

"Who's the hunk?" Rocky asked out of the corner of her mouth.

A dreamy look filled Zan's eyes. "That's Derek McClellan. He dances the Cavalier in the ballet. Isn't he beautiful?"

Mary Bubnik sighed. "Gorgeous!"

"That does it!" Gwen sucked in her stomach. "I'm starting my diet tomorrow."

A few more of the dancers from the ballet company filed into the room. Mr Anton conferred with Miss Jo for a few moments, then turned to the group. "I know it is just the first rehearsal, but I would like to share the progress of our young ballerinas with the rest of the company."

"What's that mean?" Mary Bubnik whispered to Zan.

"I think – in fact, I'm practically certain," Zan said, "that he wants us to do our dance."

"In front of him?" Gwen pointed at Derek McClellan, who was leaning easily against the dance *barre*.

"In front of everybody," Rocky said.

"I couldn't," Gwen said, shaking her head. "I'd die!"

McGee glanced at the clock. "Ten minutes left of rehearsal. If we're lucky, they won't get to us."

That hope was snuffed out as Courtney raised her hand. "Mr Anton, you really should watch the mice first." She flashed the gang a sickeningly sweet smile. "They've worked so hard this afternoon."

"She's right," Gwen blurted out. "We've worked so hard, we're exhausted."

Mr Anton chuckled, then turned to Courtney. "That's very

gracious of you, Miss Clay. I think that's a wonderful idea."

"But Mr Anton," Mary Bubnik drawled, "I'm sure the flowers' dance must be beautiful. If they went first—"

"It would truly inspire us," Zan finished.

McGee kept her eye glued to the clock. "Keep stalling," she whispered under her breath to Rocky. "Just a few more minutes and we'll be out of here."

Rocky was too busy glaring at Courtney to hear.

"Come along, girls," Miss Jo said briskly, "this is no time to be shy."

Rocky broke the silence. "Hey, it's just a dance," she said casually. "No big deal."

She stood up and walked over to the corner to take her position. As she passed by Courtney, Rocky hissed, "One more strike and you're out. Remember that."

Courtney stared back at Rocky, a tiny smile curling the edges of her mouth.

The others hurried to join Rocky. As they waited for the music to begin, Mary Bubnik repeated over and over, "Please let me get through this without falling. Please! Oh, please! Oh, please!"

Miss Bruce hit the chords that sounded like a clock ringing the hour. At the final stroke of midnight, McGee, led the others into their first step of the dance.

What followed was a total disaster. Gwen, who was right behind McGee, started too soon and then had to stop abruptly to get back in rhythm. Rocky and Zan promptly crashed into her back.

Courtney and the rest of the Bunheads started giggling. A couple of the other dancers burst out laughing. To her horror, Gwen noticed that even Derek McClellan was grinning.

Hearing the laughter made Rocky furious. She broke out of the line and started doing karate kicks in their direction. Meanwhile, Mary Bubnik, who still couldn't remember any of the steps, decided just to follow Rocky and make gruesome faces. Gwen stuck close to McGee but Zan kept sandwiching herself in between them, trying to hide from their audience.

The result was that no one could move without tripping over the other.

In a panic, McGee led them into the circle ending the dance long before their cue. The girls had no choice but to keep running around and around, waiting for the music to stop.

Every time Gwen passed by Derek McClellan she tried to suck in her stomach. On the fifth rotation, Gwen suddenly felt the effects of Hi Lo's special shake. Without warning, she was seized with a stomach cramp and bent forward, clutching her sides.

Mary Bubnik tumbled right over Gwen's back and on to the floor.

"I think I'm going to be sick!" Gwen gasped, her face a deathly green. She turned and charged for the exit.

"I'll go help her!" McGee bolted out of the room after Gwen.

Gwen raced through the lobby of the Academy with one hand clapped over her mouth. She barely made it into the bathroom. Leaping inside, she slammed the door behind her and locked it.

McGee raced to the bathroom door. Behind her she could hear the final chords of their music and then silence.

"Gwen, come out of that bathroom," McGee shouted through the locked door. "You can't stay in there forever."

"Watch me," Gwen shot back. Then she whispered, "Is rehearsal over yet?"

McGee turned and watched the dancers pouring out of the studio. "Yes, it is."

"Has he gone?"

"Who?"

"What do you mean, who?" Gwen barked. "Derek McClellan. The dancing hunk, who just witnessed the most embarrassing moment of my entire life."

"We all embarrassed ourselves," McGee reminded her.

"Then go find your own place to hide. This one is taken."

McGee heaved a huge sigh. "Come on out, Gwen, please?"

Gwen didn't respond. McGee saw Rocky, Zan, and Mary Bubnik coming towards her through the lobby.

"Is she OK?" Zan asked, her eyes full of concern.

"Yes, but she won't come out," McGee said. "She's too embarrassed."

"You think she's embarrassed?" Mary Bubnik moaned. "You should have been with us for the big finale." She leaned against the wall. "Boy, was my face red!"

"What did Mr Anton say?" McGee asked.

"Not much," Zan said. "He just kind of stared at us for a while."

"And he wasn't smiling," Rocky added. Her mouth set in a hard line as she said, "But the Bunheads were."

"Gwen?" Mary Bubnik tapped lightly on the bathroom door.

"Go away."

"Now, there's no use staying in there," Mary said through the door. "Sooner or later, you're going to have to come out."

"Never."

"Well, what are you going to do in there?"

"I'll probably waste away for a week or so, then keel over dead from starvation."

Rocky shouted over Mary' shoulder, "You'll probably die of boredom first."

"Let me try," Zan stepped up to the door. "Gwen, this is Zan. I know how awfully awful you must feel, but it's not your fault."

"It's the Bunheads' fault!" Rocky declared.

"That's exactly correct," Zan said.

Mary Bubnik leaned forward and whispered, "If you're worried about that gorgeous guy seeing you embarrass yourself – well, he didn't."

"How do you know?"

"Because when I hit the floor, I caught a glimpse of him reading a magazine."

"What?" Gwen's voice was filled with outrage. "You mean we killed ourselves, acting and dancing our brains out, and he didn't even have the courtesy to watch?"

"That's right, Gwen," McGee said.

The bathroom door flew open and hit the wall with a thunk. "I'll show him. I'll show them all."

"That's more like it!" Rocky narrowed her eyes. "And we'll start with the Bunheads."

Gwen stepped into the lobby and faced the rest of the gang. "We've got to think of a way to get back at them."

"Like putting lead weights in their flowers?" Rocky suggested. "Or maybe pins in their ballet shoes?"

Zan shook her head. "No, it has to be something wickedly clever."

"Well, what, then?" Rocky demanded.

"I don't know," Zan admitted. "But we've got a whole week to plan."

"That's right," McGee said with a grin. "And among the five of us, we should be able to think of something *good*."

Once she got home from rehearsal, Zan decided to go to the

park near her parents' apartment and finish her latest Tiffany Truenote mystery. She was right in the middle of the final chapter when an idea came to her.

"That's it!" she said. "The way to get back at the Bunheads is to let them get themselves!"

Tossing the book aside, she dug into her book bag and pulled out a sheet of paper filled with names and phone numbers. It listed everyone who was involved in *The Nutcracker*.

"Contact sheet," Zan said out loud, reading the words written across the top. She decided it was time to make contact.

Zan raced across the park back to her apartment building and ran up the stairs to the third floor. Her parents, who were both artists and taught at the Deerfield Art Institute, had converted the entire floor into an open loft apartment. The walls were covered with original paintings and textured wall hangings. Zan opened the door with her key and hurried past the paintings to her room.

Though the rest of the apartment was decorated in an ultra-modern style, Zan had insisted on having an old-fashioned bedroom. Her bed was made of polished brass and covered with a quilted comforter. Little lace pillows were neatly arranged along the headboard.

Zan sprawled across the bed and studied her contact sheet for a moment. She picked up the phone on her night stand and dialled Mary Bubnik's number. Mary lived in Glenwood, right on the edge of Deerfield, so Zan figured she would have been the first to get home from rehearsal.

The phone rang three times before a breathless voice answered, "Bubnik household, Mary speaking."

"Mary, this is Zan Reed."

"Oh, hi!" Zan heard some mumblings on Mary's end and Mary's voice saying, "It's my friend Zan from ballet."

Finally Mary came back on the line. "I wish you could see my mother's face right now," she whispered. "She is just thrilled that I have made a new friend here in Deerfield."

31

Zan giggled. She knew her parents would probably have had the same reaction if Mary had called her.

"What's up?" Mary asked.

"Well, I was pondering our desperate need for a plan while finishing the last chapter of *The Fatal Flaw*, when it hit me." Zan took a deep breath. "Have you ever heard of the saying, 'Give them enough rope, and they'll hang themselves'?"

"Yes, I believe I have," Mary Bubnik drawled. "I think it is downright gruesome." Suddenly Mary gasped. "Zan, you don't really want to—?"

"Oh, no, it just means that, if we make the right *suggestions* to Courtney and the Bunheads, they may just humiliate themselves."

There was a long pause. "I don't think I get you."

It took Zan several minutes to convince Mary to trust her scheme and just follow instructions. But when Zan called McGee, she caught on right away.

"This is great, Zan," McGee chuckled. "What do I need to do?"

"We should each go to the library and check out a couple of books about the history of ballet."

"Got it." McGee made a note to bring a large brown bag to school with her. She'd hide the books in there and that way none of her hockey teammates would ever see them. McGee had lost the courage to tell her coach about being in the ballet, and the last thing she needed was to be caught with a lot of dance books.

"You call Gwen and Rocky and tell them to do the same," Zan continued, "and then we'll all meet at the studio early on Saturday—"

"Before the Bunheads get there," McGee finished for her. "They'll never know what hit them!"

"Right!" Zan hung up the phone, picked up her stuffed brown bear and danced around the bedroom. "Well, Mr Gallagher," she said to the fuzzy toy. "It looks like we're not alone any more. We've got some friends. What do you think about that?"

Zan was answered by a gentle knock on her door.

"Zan?" A tall black woman who looked like a grown-up version of Zan stuck her head in the room. "How was ballet rehearsal?"

"Great, Mom!" Zan smiled happily. "I think we're going to win."

Mrs Reed cocked her head in confusion. "Win? I didn't realise there was a contest involved."

"Neither did we," Zan replied. "Until today."

The following Saturday, the gang came to the studio prepared. Each was loaded down with books checked out from their local library. The girls gathered in a corner of the deserted dressing room and held a hushed meeting.

Zan was delighted to see that everyone had followed her instructions to the letter. "You all look fantastically wonderful!"

McGee had wrapped her braids around her head in a neat crown. She'd even worn a pair of tights without a run in them. Mary's hair was tied in a curly pony-tail with a bright blue ribbon.

Gwen's hair was too short to do anything special with it.

33

However, she had removed her thick glasses and the transformation was startling, especially when she managed not to squint.

Rocky was the biggest surprise. She had tamed her wild mane of hair into a taut bun at the base of her neck, just like Miss Jo's. She grinned proudly. "We almost look like real bunheads." She slipped her red satin jacket on over her leotard. "Almost."

Zan, her own dark hair pulled into a neat bun like the others, said, "What's important is that the Bunheads think we're serious about ballet. Now, the first thing we should do is set the scene." Zan covered the make-up table with ballet books, propping several of them open to specific pages. "Mary, you sit here and pretend to look at the pictures."

Gwen picked up one of the books and leaned against the locker as though she were deep in thought.

"Remember," Zan whispered, "no matter what any of us says, go along with it!"

"Got it!" McGee perched on the edge of the dressing table and pretended to be engrossed in a book of her own.

Rocky, who had moved to the door to keep lookout, whistled softly. Moments later Courtney sailed into the dressing room. Page Tuttle and Alice Westcott followed close behind. Without looking at the gang, the Bunheads went straight to their usual places and began to get dressed for rehearsal.

McGee looked over at Zan and winked. That was their signal to begin.

"Oh, yes," Zan announced loudly, as if she were continuing a previous conversation, "the very, very best dancers *always* use Snowy soap flakes on their shoes, to keep from falling."

"That's amazing," Gwen said. "I thought they used rosin, like that stuff over there." She pointed to a little box sitting in the corner of the dressing room. The dancers of the Academy dipped their shoes in its sticky granules to keep from slipping.

Rocky jumped in without missing a beat. "Rosin's old hat. All of the really big New York City dancers put Snowy in their rosin boxes. It's a well-known secret. In fact, it's so popular that stores have trouble keeping it in stock."

Gwen raised an eyebrow at Rocky, as if to say, "Don't push it."

"It's easy to take care of," Zan added, "and washes right off. It says so right here in *Dance World Today*." She held up the magazine, flipping it quickly to make sure none of the Bunheads could really see the page.

McGee peeked around the corner of her book to see if Courtney was responding. McGee smiled. Courtney was hanging on to every word they were saying and so was Page Tuttle.

Zan pulled a huge box of Snowy soap flakes out of her back pack. "Here, you guys, I brought this. Feel free to use some."

"Thanks, Zan." Gwen smiled and gestured to her overstuffed blue canvas bag. "But I already have my own."

"Oooh, look at the way these dancers tie the ribbons on their toe shoes," Mary Bubnik exclaimed, pointing at a picture in her book. "Why, they lace them right up to their knees!"

"Of course," Zan said casually. "That's an age-old ballet tradition."

McGee said, "But I thought you were supposed to tie them around your ankles."

Zan shook her head. "That was before. Now all of the really good dancers crisscross them up their legs. You'll notice the dancers in that picture are in *The Nutcracker.*"

Mary overacted surprised. "Why, Zan's right! They sure are." She called over her shoulder, "Courtney, these girls are doing the *Waltz of the Flowers.*"

"Are they really?" Courtney shrugged, pretending not to care.

"Listen to this!" Gwen pretended to read from her book. "For over a hundred years, the traditions of the ballet have been handed down from generation to generation."

She paused to see how her phony speech was going over. McGee gestured for her to keep talking.

"From Pavlova's Dying Swan and the grand tradition of wearing a crown of feathers" – Gwen paused to collect her thoughts – "to the high-laced toe shoe ribbons worn by the ballerinas in the *Waltz of the Flowers* – the greatness continues!"

The gang turned to look at Courtney, who was taking a very long time to adjust her hair in the mirror.

"Boy, I sure envy you guys," Mary Bubnik declared with a loud sigh. "Getting to wear toe shoes and lacing your ribbons up high like that."

"Like real ballerinas," McGee agreed.

Courtney smiled at her reflection in the mirror. They could see she felt flattered.

"Well, maybe someday," Courtney said with a regal wave of her hand, "you, too, will get to wear toe shoes. I wouldn't count on it, though."

Zan nodded sadly. "I guess we'll have to be content to only dream of becoming a *real* ballerina – like you, Courtney." Zan rolled her eyes and McGee had to smother a giggle with her hand.

Courtney did a couple of stretches, aware that she was being watched. She reached gracefully to the ceiling then bent forward and when her nose touched her knees, she declared, "Practice makes perfect."

"That's true." Rocky motioned for the others to pick up their books and follow her. "Guess we'd better go on into the studio. I sure hope we can squeeze in a little extra practice on our mouse dance."

They walked as casually as they could out of the dressing room and into the studio. Rocky led them to the far side of the classroom where they burst into giggles.

"Do you think the plan will work?" McGee asked, her cheeks flushed with excitement.

"We'll know as soon as we see their toe shoe ribbons," Zan replied.

"If they fall for that," Gwen chortled, "then they'll fall for the soap flakes and put Snowy in the resin box."

"Now, if anything happens," Rocky said quickly, "I want you guys to remember, keep a poker face!"

"A poker face?" Mary Bubnik repeated. "What's that?"

"This." Rocky stared straight ahead without putting any expression on her face. "People do it when they play cards," she explained. "That way no one can guess what they're thinking or what cards they have in their hands."

They all faced the large mirror and tried out various blank expressions.

There was a sudden commotion at the door to the studio and a jumble of voices could be heard outside.

Miss Jo and Mrs Bruce entered the room first, followed by Mr Anton and various members of the ballet company.

"All right, we have a lot to do today, and very little time," Mr Anton announced. "So we will go through the dances one by one, beginning with the *Waltz of the Flowers*."

Miss Jo clapped her hands. "Dancers, take your positions, please!"

The dancers of the *corps de ballet* of the Academy consisted of twelve girls in their late teens. They were to be joined in the *Waltz of the Flowers* by the younger dancers, led by Courtney Clay.

"Cross your fingers, everybody," Gwen whispered. "Here come the Bunheads!"

First the older girls waltzed in a line across the room. Then came Courtney, smiling beautifully as she danced.

The fist sign of anything unusual was the trail of white footprints left behind her as she crossed the studio floor.

Snickers went around the room as other dancers noticed the pretty pink satin ribbons she had carefully wrapped around her calves up to her knee. Behind her, Page and Alice and a few of the other Flowers had done the same.

McGee jabbed Gwen in the side. "It worked!"

"Shhh!" Rocky hushed her. The five girls sat quietly in their corner and waited for the fun to begin.

More and more white footprints appeared until soon the wooden floor was almost covered with them.

"Uh-oh," Rocky whispered as the girls doubled back for a diagonal cross. "Here it comes."

Page leaped out confidently. The foot she landed on hit the white flakes and shot out from under her. She reached out blindly and clutched at Courtney's arm. The two of them collapsed in a heap, just as the rest of the girls began to slip and slide behind them.

Mrs Bruce stopped playing. Several of the older dancers rushed on to the floor to help the girls. Within seconds they were flailing around helplessly. No one could get enough traction to stand up.

"Wowie!" was all McGee could say.

"They look like skaters in slow motion," Gwen whispered.

"I hope no one's hurt," Mary Bubnik said.

"Naw." Rocky shook her head. "Just surprised."

Finally one of the girls crawled on her hands and knees to the *barre* and pulled herself up to a standing position. One by one the others did the same. Within minutes order had returned to the room and a furious Mr Anton turned on Courtney and her companions.

"What is the meaning of this?" he demanded. "What have you put on your shoes?"

One of the older dancers touched the white powder on the floor and rubbed her fingers. "I think this is soap."

"Soap!" Mr Anton turned to Courtney. "What possessed you to put soap on your shoes?"

"I-I'm sorry," Courtney mumbled.

"We thought that—" Page began, then finished lamely, "We didn't know."

Courtney shot an angry look at the gang. Rocky hissed, "Poker face!"

Immediately they stared straight ahead. Not a glimmer of emotion showed on their faces.

It was hard. Gwen really wanted to laugh. She bit her cheek, which only brought tears to her eyes.

"And those ribbons! Is this a joke?" Mr Anton pointed at the laced ribbons that had tumbled down around their ankles. "You shouldn't have toe shoes unless you know how to wear them."

"Anton, I'm sure the girls meant no harm," Miss Jo said, putting her hand on his shoulder to calm him down.

"It's unbelievable," he fumed. "This dance floor is a mess of soap flakes. We can't rehearse here. They have completely ruined our afternoon."

Miss Jo led him over the piano, gesturing for Courtney and the rest of the flowers to quietly leave the studio.

"This is everything we could have hoped for," Gwen whispered, "And more."

The Bunheads never came back. Miss Jo took the mice to Studio B and ran through their dance quickly, then dismissed them early.

When the gang left Hillberry Hall, they found an angry Courtney Clay waiting for them on the steps.

"No one, but no one, humiliates Courtney Clay," she hissed through clenched teeth. "You little rats are going to regret this. I mean it."

Before anyone could reply, she stalked off down the steps.

"Boy, oh, boy," Mary Bubnik muttered. "Those sound like fighting words to me."

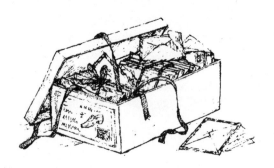

PULLING UP THE OLD SOCKS

LYNN SEYMOUR with Paul Gardner

from Lynn – the autobiography of Lynn Seymour

At the age of fifteen Berta Lynn Springbett left her home in Canada to take up a place at the Sadler's Wells Ballet School in London (now the Royal Ballet School). Later, under her stage name Lynn Seymour, she became one of the Royal Ballet's greatest stars.

LITTLE PATCHES of farms and ribbons of roads seen through oceans of clouds from an aeroplane window – that was my first glimpse of England when I arrived in the fall of 1954. My farewell flowers, a bouquet of red roses, drooped lifelessly and I drooped with them, although the roses had been put on ice for part of the trip and Dad had given me a sleeping pill. I tried to remain very ladylike and calm, but I wished that I could have been put on ice with the roses. Midway over the Atlantic I had a nasty shock. The full realization hit that I was going to be dropped in a foreign country, without any relatives around for weekends or holiday visits. At the age of fifteen, I was not popping off three hours away by train from my parents. I was starting ballet school six thousand miles from home and I would be living with strangers. The night before I left Vancouver, Mom and Dad and I saw *Gone With the Wind* which now struck me as an awesomely prophetic title. I wanted to grab the roses and bail out. Instead I remained strapped in my seat, while the pubescent heart did flip-flops, clutching the flowers which I presented to my stand-in mom, Phyllis Fisher, of 28 Orsett Terrace, Paddington. I wore a new grey suit and red shoes, a silk scarf and white gloves. To fake a maturity I did not feel or have, I had boarded the plane carrying a hat shaped like a sponge cake, with a veil. A stewardess who chatted with me about my adventurous expedition gasped when she saw me adjusting the veil over my left eye. The British, it had been drilled into me, were quite proper, so what could be more proper than a hat, even though it made me look like a miscast dowager in a school play. "I wouldn't wear that hat," the stewardess said. "You're not going to a funeral." I left the grey velour sponge cake at Heathrow Airport.

A teacher from the Sadler's Wells School in Barons Court greeted me at the aircoach terminal, after a jittery bus ride into central London during which I stared straight ahead, forcing myself not to cry, and I was deposited at the Fishers' door in Paddington, a rather dreary area with faded houses and a few scraggly trees. London seemed so enormous and sprawling, with streams of people hurrying in every direction, and the streets clogged with buses, taxis and cars. There were no snow-capped mountains and sandy beaches. I was alone in the first big city I had ever seen, and there was no turning back. The lump in my throat was the size of a golf ball. Orsett Terrace was my new berth – the first of temporary boarding houses, bed-sits, flats, digs, lodgings and hotels for the next seventeen years of suitcase living, until I could afford to buy my own home in the suburb of Chiswick. When I stepped across the threshold and quiveringly gave Mrs Fisher the roses, I did not believe that I would ever remain long in London.

Phyllis Fisher was a small, rather shy woman with a pleasant face, in her late forties who constantly bustled. She had been a nurse during the war and continued hospital duties for a short time after her son Jeremy was born. Jeremy was eleven. She and her husband inherited a four-storey house and rented rooms to foreign students, usually teenage girls from France who were studying English for a year. There were always one or two English girls enrolled at the ballet school. Mrs Fisher did not take in boys, though that would have been more matey for Jeremy. Boys were mischievous and cheeky, she said, and did not like kitchen work. She provided breakfast, dinner and a room for four pounds four shillings a week. The girls set the table and washed up the dishes. We were also responsible for tidying our rooms. But Mrs Fisher did everything else. She shopped for a "family" of seven or eight, trudging to markets and greengrocers four times a week; she planned her menus as carefully as a hospital cook. Rationing was only just over and it was difficult to satisfy French and Canadian palates. She also listened to the woes of her boarders and worried about them, which is why she preferred older girls, aged seventeen or eighteen: they had fewer adjustment problems. Sometimes, she remarked with a heavy sigh, it was easier being a nurse than running a boarding house, but she did not want to be on her feet all day tending grumbling patients and she had seen enough death during the war. She swapped the bedpan for the frying pan and pressed on with her lot in life. When boarders became tearful, she comforted them with the no-nonsense authority of a Head Nurse ordering a patient to gulp down his medicine: "You simply have to pull up the old socks." I was her youngest boarder. My scholarship gave me free instruction at the ballet school and two pounds a week towards my board. And Mrs Fisher was forever telling me to pull up the old socks.

When my son Addie commented on my huge box of letters, I jokingly asked if he read the juicy parts. There were no juicy parts, ever. The early letters were most often wet, as in full of tears. I repressed the dislocation of that first year. But the letters are vignettes of me, revealing far more than I could today of the young Berta Lynn Springbett, someone I tried to toss off later in a tumbler of sophistication.

Selected samples from those first months – candid verbal portraits of a girl I still remember:

September 5

Dear Mom,

I don't think I can stand it for a year. I miss you so much I could just fly home right now. It was childish of me, asking you to sleep with me the last night, but you calmed me down. Everything is Merrie in Olde England except me. The Fishers are trying to help me get over my homesickness and say I will feel lots better when the other girls arrive. Mr Fisher works for the government housing projects, listening to sob stories of homeless people. My first night here he had to listen to me. I explained how badly I felt and he consoled me no end. But, Mom, only me going home or your coming here can help me.

My room, on the top floor, is a little bigger than at home. I have a bed, a desk, a little dressing-table, a sink, an easy chair and a bureau. I gave Mrs Fisher my roses, but they were dead, and she put a vase of fresh daisies in my room. That was very sweet. For dinner the first night we had veal or something. Actually I am not sure what it was and did not want to ask. After dinner we watched TV, but each minute I got more homesick wanting you, till, by the time I was to go to bed, I was ready to die. I stood at the window a long time staring into the street. The houses in Orsett Terrace are all alike with

thousands of chimneys on each roof. The district is not very pretty. I think we got Kensington mixed up with Paddington.

I heard the bells toll two. I don't know what time I finally dropped off. I had a terrible sleep. I am saving Dad's second sleeping pill for the Big Emergency, but I think it is here. Oh, Mom, please get me away. If you only knew how urgent I am.

All my love to you,

Lynn

September 8

Dearest Mom,

If you can't get me away before summer then I will have to stay but you must get me away or I will do something drastic. I receive piles of letters, but you must keep writing. The letters make me more homesick, but I feel so much closer to you. Do try to get me home with all your heart. I took Dad's second sleeping pill and that made me feel better. I dread going to bed at night because I get so lonely for you, but what is worse is waking up in the morning.

I am trying to accustom myself to London. On Saturday I went to the bank and got everything fixed up. Then I went to Cyril Beaumont's Book Shop where I bought a subscription to *Dance and Dancers* and a book on Sadler's Wells. Mr Beaumont signed the book for me. He is a dance historian and critic. I took a long bus ride. Mr Fisher said the way to see London is from the top of a double-decker bus. The problem is you just don't pay one fare. The conductor asks, "Where are you getting off?" I told him I didn't know. He said I had to be going somewhere because my fare depended on that. So I said, "Buckingham Palace," and he said the bus didn't go there. Then I said, "Piccadilly Circus," and he answered that would be fine. I saw all the theatres and clubs and flashy restaurants in Piccadilly, where the traffic is wild, and walked to Trafalgar Square – you know, with all the pigeons and the fountain and the Lord Nelson column. I even walked past the Royal Opera House in Covent Garden and peeked in the stage door. Covent Garden itself is a marketplace. There is nothing around that makes you think of a theatre except the opera house. It is terribly grand. Then I bought some ballet cards. They were so lovely, in colour, I couldn't resist them. I stuck them into the frame of my bedroom mirror. I bought cards of Margot Fonteyn in *Swan Lake* and Svetlana Beriosova, also in *Swan Lake*. Beriosova is only twenty-two and began dancing at the Garden three years ago. She is very aristocratic-looking and I can hardly wait to see her dance. She was born in Lithuania. Just knowing that makes me feel less like a hick in London. I had to explain what a "hick" was to Mr Fisher. He said, "Oh, you mean country bumpkin."

Leaving the card shop, I got a bit confused about where to go, so I went up to one of those British gentlemen with their handle-bar moustaches and asked him which way to Charing Cross Road. He then gave me a withering look and said, "Madam, you are walking in the wrong direction." Did I turn red! I bought some Kleenex and a roll of toilet paper. The kind the Fishers have is rather like paper for dress patterns. In fact the toilets themselves are so odd. You have to pull a little chain or string. It was dark when I got home to the Fishers and Jane had arrived. She studies at the Ballet school too, but her parents live only a few hours away in Birmingham. Her parents had just left and I suddenly felt a strange twinge. Mrs Fisher said she'd ring the school and get me passes for Covent Garden. Right now I would do anything to see you. If you only knew how urgent I am.

All my love to you,
Lynn

September 15

Dearest Mom,

On Monday I trundled off to school full of excitement. Once I'm inside the school I am in a dancer's paradise. I am not homesick. For the first two weeks we have nothing but dancing. We were measured for our class uniform. We get a grey tunic and trunks, and pink knitted tights and a sort of wraparound sweater (we can buy them from the school). We

45

received a dark red belt and headband. The headband makes my face as round as a billiard ball. Then we were given assigned places in the school dressing-rooms. I didn't know anyone. The girls are funny. "Oh, darling!" and "Jolly good!" are their favourite expressions.

I can't seem to do anything in dance class. I wobble all over the place. Everyone else is so good, I feel quite lost and inferior. After one class I worked about forty minutes by myself because I can't seem to get my head and body facing the right way at the same time. Then I found out we are not allowed to do any unsupervised practice. We had our first mime class. We're not supposed to put any feeling into it until we learn the complete vocabulary and do each movement-gesture correctly. My favourite expressions are fear and anger because they require subtlety without looking ridiculous. Mime is truly an art form – conveying all the emotions without words.

At the end of the day, we had foot inspection. We have to rub our feet with surgical spirit and powder them before and after class, and also powder our shoes. At night we have to bathe our feet in hot water, and rub them with surgical spirit and lanolin. Finally we must take a nail file and push down the cuticle of our toe nails and powder *them*. As soon as I return to the Fishers, I proceed to darn point shoes. We have to darn toes and all the little spots where the satin is likely to wear away. A tough linen thread is used on the heel and ball of the foot. Last night I struggled along and finally finished one shoe. The boys do not have to darn, because they are never on point. It seems as if I will spend my whole life darning shoes.

Two French girls are at the Fishers' now. They are twenty and learning English. They absolutely refuse to speak any English at the dinner table. They just talk to each other in French. The dining room and kitchen at the Fishers' are on the basement level and the shower is there too. It is the warmest part of the house. I have a little radiator in my room and it goes on after you insert a shilling and light a match. The heat stays on a couple of hours, then you must repeat the process. It is icy and pitch black outside when I wake and I must remember to keep the stack of shillings and little matchboxes on my bureau. I was preparing to get into bed and had just put a shilling in the radiator when, suddenly, I felt an odd little spasm again. Then I heard a huge wail, like a baby or lost child. It was so pitiful and I was sure someone was crying. I ran into the hall and looked around. Jane was coming out of the bathroom and she said that I had heard a "London cat". They are homeless and roam all over the city. She begged me not to worry. She came into my room and we talked about school. This is her third year. She is nice, but quite shy and the only boarder I can chat with. I said that I was very impressed with my dance teacher Winifred Edwards, a wonderful woman about sixty years old. Her hair is chalk white, parted in the middle and marcelled. She wears impeccable white shoes and her dresses are usually green and white, with flared skirts. She has lovely legs. Jane said that Winifred Edwards used to be known as Vera Fredova and, as a young girl, danced with the Anna Pavlova company. This was in the days when dancers had to have Russian names. The Russian impresario, Sergei Diaghilev, had many English girls in his troupe. Hilda Munnings changed her name to Lydia Sokolova and Lilian Alicia Marks became Alicia Markova. But that was years ago. Don't worry. I won't have to change my name. Winifred Edwards (Vera Fredova) met a Diaghilev dancer and his wife who formed a company back in 1917. She toured the United States with them and ended up in Hollywood where everything fell apart. Miss Edwards was told to hold on, there would be another tour, but there never was and she was stuck in Hollywood. Isn't that awful? She taught dancing there and one of her students was the choreographer Agnes de Mille. By the time Miss Edwards returned to England, it was too late for her to pursue a ballet career. I'm so lucky to have her for a teacher. I think she retires next year. She is very fierce at times but she has a marvellous dance history which I respect. When Jane left my room I lay in bed under mountains of blankets thinking of Miss Edwards. The story of her being stranded in California, yet still hopeful until the end, is so sad that it gave me the blubs. When she demonstrates a step I then see the lithesome young Vera Fredova. Jane says, "People forget dancers, even the great ones, very quickly." I don't think she expects to make it, but I want to. I just have to hold on, don't I?

All my love,
Lynn

September 16

Dear Dad,

I am gradually settling down (I think), though we won't have a regular routine until next week when we start academic subjects as well. The headmistress asked what courses I wanted to take and I said, "Everything." I just finished a ballet class, which is what I look forward to. I am now five foot four inches and Winifred Edwards said, "That is a good height, do not grow any taller." When girls stand on point we gain about two inches and therefore it is best to be on the short side. It also makes it easier for the boys to fling us around. The boys have separate classes. They have to learn speed and strength like track stars. A difference is that when they leap, they're holding on to one of us instead of a pole vault, so they better know what they're doing.

You would like Mr Fisher. When I get the blues he is very patient. He is a bit on the portly side, wears thick glasses and has a moustache. He looks exactly like Groucho Marx. His opinion of the ballet is the same as yours. "I like it all right," he says, "but I don't care if I see it or not." He is interested in sports – cricket, soccer, rugby. Of course I lectured Mr Fisher and stressed that ballet gives boys stronger muscular development and body coordination than any sport.

Did I tell you what happened to my watch? Here's a "London story". I lost the crystal and one of the hands snapped off. Mr Fisher sent me to a wee little shop in Paddington. A strange fat lady was there seated at a rolltop desk. She must have weighed two hundred pounds and I wondered how she squeezed in and out of the doorway because it was so tiny. You have to go down several steps to get into the shop. Inside the shop were five yapping poodles, all with diamond-studded leather collars. I even saw one black poodle with a gold clip in its topknot. I thought perhaps I was in a weird kennel instead of a watch repair shop. Every five minutes different clocks would start chiming or ringing or going cuckoo-cuckoo. The fat lady wore several watches on her arms like bracelets and a diamond-studded collar around *her* neck. Mr Fisher said, "She's quaint." I think there are a lot of odd characters in London other than wailing London cats. Eccentricity is tolerated here far more than at home.

It was very reassuring that you wrote again that you are behind me all the time. It made me feel one hundred per cent better. Please remember, you are not just a "bread-winner" to me. You are the most wonderful father anyone could have. You are working to keep me in London in order that I can do what I want with my life.

All my love,
Lynn

September 28

Dearest Mom,

We've started the full academic-dance schedule at school. I have French three times a week and English, Greek history, art appreciation, history of the ballet and music once a week. The other classes are involved with dance – pirouette, mime, point, character dancing, and ballet every day with Winifred Edwards. We are learning the *corps de ballet* sections of *Swan Lake*, Act 2. I'm up at seven-thirty every morning to be at school by nine-fifteen and we are finished at five o'clock. I'm not getting the education I would at home, and this worries me, but I am trying to make up for it by reading a lot. I have become friendly with a Brazilian girl named Marcia Haydée Pereira da Silva. She calls herself Marcia Haydée. She is seventeen and began dancing when she was three, like all well-bred girls in Rio. She had no interest in dolls or games, something we have in common. And then she saw *The Red Shoes*, and it changed her life. We talked about *The Red Shoes* for hours. She met the director at a dinner party given by her parents and he encouraged her to attend our school. She knows that she won't be able to graduate into the company because she is not a resident of a Commonwealth country, but she is very determined and works quite hard. I usually stand behind her when we are doing our *pliés* at the *barre*, up-down, up-down, bending our knees with our feet turned out. I wear woolly tights but some mornings my cold bones make a crunching noise when I start the *pliés*.

Marcia and I are "outsiders", the other girls seldom notice us. Marcia has long black hair and is about an inch shorter than me. She has a long lovely neck, a swan neck, unlike me. I have to concentrate on the use of my neck since I can't have it stretched.

Marcia and I went for snacks in a very posh department store. I worry about my expenses, but I did want to go with her so very much. A paunchy man, standing in a tail coat and pinstripe trousers with a carnation in his lapel, showed us to a table. The room had a red carpet and chandeliers. The waitresses wore white organdy aprons. I tried to be as nonchalant as Marcia. We had passes to Covent Garden. After coffee and sandwiches with olives and watercress, we took our passes to the stage door and exchanged them for a proper ticket. Then we went around to the front and dashed up to the Stalls Circle to get a decent place to stand without a pole in front of us. We saw *Les Sylphides* with Anne Heaton. She was marvellous. On the same programme was *Firebird*. Margot Fonteyn danced the firebird who helps the prince rescue an enchanted princess. It was a magnificent production with Fonteyn an exotic firebird and Svetlana Beriosova absolutely breathtaking as the princess. The other ballet was *La Boutique Fantasque*, about a bunch of toys that come to life, and I don't know why the Garden has it in the repertoire. We saw Winifred Edwards at the end of the performance and had a nice chat with her, although Marcia thought that I shouldn't have said the last ballet was dreadful. Miss Edwards just smiled. I suspect she agreed with me.

On Monday Miss Edwards sent me home after class. I developed a horrid cold and have a constantly runny nose. But I don't like to stay in bed by myself on the top floor because it is so lonely. I much prefer being around people, even if they don't talk to me, like the girls at school (not Marcia, of course!). It is also very chilly in my room. So the very next day I went to school again and Miss Edwards sent me home again. She phoned Mrs Fisher and urged her to make me stay in bed. My body aches and I have a burning head. Naturally I ran out of shillings for my little heater. I gave Jeremy Fisher a pound note and he sweetly left an envelope of shillings outside my door on a tray with hot tea and barley soup. Oh, Mom, I was expecting to hear you come to the door and make me feel better with a big hug. I wanted you so much.

      All my love,
      Lynn

P.S. Don't forget to send vitamins, instant coffee and Breck shampoo.

October 12

Dearest Mom and Dad,

Went to school wearing two sweaters and mufflers. It was freezing cold. I got so upset in dance class that I just about cried. I feel absolutely lost and so far behind everyone. After class I was walking toward the dressing-rooms and the tears started to flow, and who should come along but Miss Edwards. I was so embarrassed. I just told her the truth – my body is stubby and I am shaky. She said very curtly, "Nonsense. You're doing quite well." That made me feel better. She told me to get more sleep as I was looking pale. This was the first time I've had anybody express concern about me since I got here and that sure was nice.

I saw Margot Fonteyn take theatre class. I watched her at the *barre*. Fonteyn wore a great long-sleeved kind of pink sweater tied in the middle with a yellow cord, and pink tights. Her hair was pinned up. She was so graceful, so utterly lovely, I just gaped. There is nothing at all "grand" about Fonteyn. She does not put on airs. Her grace is effortless, unaffected, without bravura. Her lively dark eyes are luminous. Her face is slightly heart-shaped and she has a light olive skin. Her total dedication is only noticed in the firmness of her mouth. Mine just quivers. The school has a big box of old point shoes that you can buy, for practising. I was rummaging through, found a pair my size and tried them on. They were fine. I turned them over and whose name should I see on them but Fonteyn's!

I love theatre class, but sometimes my body wants to do funny things and I'm afraid to "let go". We are learning that arm movements are just as important as what we do with our feet. The movements cannot be contrived posturings but rather part of a delicate, fluid "line". I like to put some flesh-and-blood into each detail and gesture.

Yesterday I was invited out by a girl at school I do not really like or admire, but accepted her invitation because it was so thoughtful of her to ask me. She lives at a Catholic hostel and she didn't introduce me to anybody. All she did was talk about how much she disliked the school and our dance teacher Miss Edwards. She called her a dictator! Anyway she put me in a dark mood, like the time I chased Bruce around the house with a knife for teasing me. I was angry with myself for having anything to do with a girl who said such hateful things, and, besides, she lived in a place where the older girls smoked!

I waited in the Standing Room line at the Garden for three hours on Saturday to buy a ticket (six shillings) for *Coppélia* with the radiant Svetlana Beriosova. During the intervals I wandered around the foyer and "crush bar", a bit like an orphan at a palace party. I was so thirsty I ordered a glass of lemonade. I ran into Miss Edwards during the second interval. She noticed my sweaty brow and bought me an ice cream. She says I've got to relax more. I'm nervous because I am definitely gaining weight. Instead of filling up on an apple or pear, like I do at home, I fill up on bread. We don't get too much meat at the Fishers', but I now try to eat gobs of cheese and an egg every day for breakfast. I did have one excellent meal at the Royal Festival Hall when I attended a Beethoven concert with Marcia Haydée. A melon cocktail, baked chicken with veggies and a green salad. We really paid for it, though. It cost twelve shillings. That is about $1.68. It is a lot for England and a lot for me. But a little splurge makes life at the Fishers' more bearable. The thing is I know Mrs F. does the best she can.

We celebrated the birthday of one of the French girls who turned twenty-one. She still refuses to speak English, so we just do a lot of "Áa-va-ing", which is a tiresome form of conversation. Mr Fisher surprised us with a bottle of champagne. POP! My first glass of champagne. I quite liked it.

Love,
Lynn

November 14

Dearest Mom,

Ever since I got your letter I have been on a tight economy drive. I now itemize every expense. It's a matter of learning how to deal with money. I told Marcia Haydée I could not eat lunch any more at Mrs Honeybun's. Mrs Honeybun has a little café near the school and we went there for roast beef sandwiches. The school lunches are quite OK, only two shillings, about thirty cents. There are always puddings and custards. I try not to eat them because they make me fat. The sight of so many thick puddings and custards turns me quite gooey inside. My face and arms and waist are filling out. But I did have a fine dance class with Miss Edwards, who said, "Very *nice*, Springbett." It made the day for me. She was in a rage at some of the girls and snapped at them. I felt sorry for those who are getting it. Her advice is always good. "Hold your neck and shoulders as if you're wearing diamonds you want everyone to see," she commands.

After French class I got dressed for point class and I could not find my point shoes anywhere. I hunted high and low. My shoes were missing. I was nearly in hysterics. Marcia found them just as class began. They were in a corner, under a towel. Marcia says one of the girls must have hidden them. It seems so odd! You have no idea what a panicky feeling I had. And of course I was late for class. The dance classes are exhausting, but I've improved my arms – they have more feeling in them, they are not just weights hanging from my shoulders. I am also developing a stronger sense of balance. My tendons may be sore, but they are flexible.

When I reached Orsett Terrace, around six o'clock, pushed along by a torrent of chilly air, I was so tired I couldn't face climbing the four flights to my room. I just sat on the first steps for ten minutes. Jeremy brought me a cup of hot tea and said his Mom had a surprise for me, but I wouldn't know what it was until breakfast. When I awoke and came downstairs I found a tiny muffin sitting on my plate. I had told Mrs F. about your muffins and she made them from the recipe off the Bran box. Then your letter came. Hearing about the mountains and Dad washing the car, and bacon & eggs just made me feel I was looking out our bathroom window and I could hear the bacon sizzle. Sometimes when I wash my

face and my eyes are closed I pretend that I'm in our bathroom and just have to go down the hall to my bedroom. I must be an odd little whatnot. Miss Edwards calls me "little whatnot".

On Sunday I went to Hampton Court Palace where Henry VIII used to live. The grounds, with the fountains and shrubs and perfect lawns, took me into a historic storybook setting. Saw the old kitchen and wine cellar, the great hall with its massive stained glass windows and vast bedrooms. I also visited the Tower of London where Henry VIII chopped off the heads of two Queens. I was by myself and getting that funny spasm again, but when I thought about prisoners facing death I forgot the spasm. Mrs Fisher says I must concentrate on things other than you, but I don't think she had executions in mind. I'm surprised Henry VIII didn't drown one of his wives in a gigantic vat of custard. That surely would be the worst torture. I also spent some hours at the National Art Gallery. I particularly liked a painting by Rubens of a girl in a felt hat, though the painting is called *The Straw Hat*. The girl has a pure roundish face, big eyes and a full bosom. The portrait, done in opulent colours, is very intense and sensual. The face and eyes sort of reminded me of me.

Last week I went to the Sadler's Wells Theatre (part of the Royal Opera House organization) and saw a new ballet, *Café des Sports*. It was about a bike race in France. Only mildly interesting. I did enjoy watching a lanky dancer in purple tights who played an Existential artist, Kenneth MacMillan – he is also a choreographer. He has great big flashing legs and soft undulating movements. The interval was most dramatic. I spotted Ninette de Valois, Empress of the British Ballet. She is a smallish woman, married to a doctor, whose vivid presence makes her loom very large. I am fearful of the day when she attends a class because she can be quite critical. She started her career in her teens, touring seaside resorts. Of those early days she once said, "Not only have I danced on every pier, I have also been hissed off every music hall stage

in England." She sounds fiercely irresistible! She is known affectionately as Madam. Some dancers call her the Dame, a title given to her by Queen Elizabeth.

I'm dreading Xmas. Do you know what I'd really like? A Christmas stocking. Would you fill one up and send it to me? In the same package could you also send my rhinestone bracelet, Avon's perfumed deodorant (To a Wild Rose), Kleenex, my camera, bobby pins and sugar cubes. Jeremy Fisher has never seen sugar cubes and I want to show him what they are like. But, most of all for Xmas, I'd like a phone call.

I'm feeling much better but I get awfully tired of having so much responsibility, especially the handling of expenses. (I only spent ten pounds last month.) I don't get so homesick, except in the mornings when I wake up, and need you so badly, Mom. Having someone who cares for you deeply, who always has a shoulder, like yours, is what I miss.

Finally, before my heater goes off and I have to insert another shilling, I must tell you about an extraordinary incident at the Garden. I received a pass to the Paris Opera Ballet and wore my black taffeta skirt and black blouse. The ballet was about a Degas dancer and an Apollo statue that came to life in a museum. WELL – the ballerina threw up on stage. I was not sure what had happened, but she made a jolting gesture and ran off. A man with opera glasses told me during the interval. Imagine, throwing up on the stage at Covent Garden!

Lots of love,

Lynn

I turned sixteen in March and did not feel different, except that I was rounder. I had an operation, or "manipulation", on a troubled left foot and woke up in a strange ward to an anvil chorus of feminine snores. For several minutes I did not know where or who I was. "You mustn't be depressed," Miss Edwards said. "If you have the courage, you can make it." One day Dame Ninette de Valois came to dance class. She sat very regally, glacially on a chair and observed. When she smiled at me, her eyes penetrating every bone in my body, my heart seemed to stop. Every summer teachers from all over the world gathered at the school for a demonstration of the dance syllabus – technical tests required to pass the school's dance examination. I was among two or three girls asked to participate in the demonstration. Miss Edwards was worried about my footwork and didn't want me to demonstrate a certain exercise. "What do you mean, she's not strong enough?" Madam asked suspiciously. She ordered me on: "Do them, please." When I finished she said, "Splendid. Not strong enough? *You see!*"

I was encouraged by Arnold Haskell, Miss Edwards and Madam, but, at the end of each day, when I took two underground trains to Paddington, to the boarding house on Orsett Terrace, where I existed solely on news from home and continued to disturb my parents with letters of loneliness, the odd spasms consumed me. My parents finally put it to me straightaway: I would have to decide before packing up for the summer whether I wanted to return to the school. I spent an afternoon wandering sightlessly through the green fields of Hyde Park and stumbled back to the greyness of Orsett Terrace at twilight. I skipped dinner and remained in my room, eating raisins and apples sent from Canada, while preparing to pull up the old socks. I even bought a bottle of turquoise ink for the momentous occasion. The letter is in my hand. The ink has not faded, the tissue-thin blue paper is still crisp.

Dear Mom and Dad,

I received your two-page letter and was very much disturbed by the decision you asked. I was hoping that everything was going to be taken for granted. My answer is – I want to return to London and the school. I've thought about it very carefully. I know that when I return from my trip home I shall feel homesick again and I will have quite a time talking myself out of it. But I'm sure I will get over it more quickly. Oh, Mom, it breaks my heart to make this decision, but I want to be a dancer and it's not possible to be one at home in Vancouver. If I said – right, I'll stay at home and be a normal 100 per cent redblooded Canadian schoolgirl, after a month I'd be weeping and wailing and gnashing my teeth and would never ever forgive myself for giving up this opportunity. Being away from home and people you love is a sacrifice a dancer simply has to make. I would never forgive myself if I gave up this chance. If I stayed at home and was miserable, you would be unhappy too. But if you knew I was doing the thing I love and want to give my life for, you would be happy too.

> Love,
> Lynn

LUCY JANE AND THE RUSSIAN BALLET

SUSAN HAMPSHIRE

Lucy Jane and her ballet school friends have come to Moscow to study for a few weeks at the Hirkov Ballet School. To add to the excitement, a video is being made of their dancing for Russian television.

O N THE DAY of the recording the atmosphere at the ballet school was electric. Children and teachers alike were rushing up and down corridors with costumes, headdresses and sheets of music. Cameras and lighting equipment were in the main studio and electric cables were strewn everywhere.

Lucy Jane joined all the other children in the dining room, where they had been asked to meet after an early breakfast. She had her little mascot bear in a plastic bag with her ballet shoes, hairbrush and hair clips. She felt slightly light-headed. At last the pain of struggling to achieve perfection, of forcing her body to perform the difficult movements Miss Marova wanted, would be put to the test.

What she was most excited about was the *pas de deux* with Marie. This would really be her chance to show how much she had learnt, and give her an opportunity to shine. The first dance to be recorded was the *Gopak*. The children were

60

hurriedly getting into costumes and doing their hair, when Miss Marova announced, "I have news for you, the principal of the school will watch you perform today."

The Russian children were tremendously excited about this.

Lucy Jane and the English children had not seen the principal since the first day, when she had told them to be prepared to suffer. To them she was just a shadowy figure in black, and did not represent the impressive figure she did to the Russian boys and girls.

When Miss Marova had gone Karina and Anna said excitedly to Lucy Jane and Marie, "Madame Krotchenova to watch. Wonderful! Principal of school much important."

Marie and Lucy Jane looked suitably impressed but Miss Marova had become their mentor, their inspiration, the most important person in their dancing lives. What they didn't know was that the principal of the Hirkov Ballet School was one of the most influential and important figures in Russian ballet. She could make or break a young dancer's career.

When the children were ready, the small group in the Russian folk dance went into the main studio, which had huge drapes all round the room to hide the mirrors and black-out the windows. The studio was ablaze with lights and cameras, technicians and assistants, shouting and running in every direction.

Miss Marova was talking to the TV director, her hands expressing the movements of the dance, but the principal was nowhere to be seen, much to the Russian children's disappointment. "Childrens," Miss Marova said, her eyes shining with excitement. "This is the director, Boris Tolstoy. You will rehearse the *Gopak* once for the director and camera, then we make video."

The children quickly ran to their places to start, while the pianist practised the music.

Miss Marova walked up to the waiting children and said, "Today is the moment we have worked many weeks for with heart and blood. Today is the day I want all pupils to give me all their heart when they dance. I want to see you dance with

61

the joy of life. Dance to make your hard work look easy. I want you to make me happy when you dance." She looked at them all in turn and said quietly, "I love all you childrens because you love my love, dance. Now you show me you love me and dance with your feet and heart." The children nodded. Anna had tears in her eyes and Natasha rushed to kiss Miss Marova's hand in a gesture of admiration and gratitude.

Miss Marova looked at the director, he looked at the pianist and the music began and the children started. The boys and girls moved from either side, their red boots clicking on the floor as they glided into the centre of the studio taking their partners as they danced. The boys with one hand on their hips, their other stretched out to take the girl by the waist and whirl her around. The children's feet neatly danced the steps together and perfectly in time. As they spun, the girls' skirts swung out, their petticoats showing. Each child holding their partner by the waist, facing each other, hip to hip, and spinning joyously, their arms held out to the side.

"Stop, stop, stop," the director suddenly shouted just as the children really thought the dance was going well. Miss Marova looked cross. "What's the problem?" she asked.

"No problem," Boris Tolstoy replied smiling, in perfect English. "I want to watch the dance from the caravan and see it on camera," and he left the studio to go down into the video recording van, where on small screens he could see all the pictures that each camera was taking. There he could decide how he was going to compose his shots and which camera would be used for filming which part of the dance.

The children were relieved that it was nothing to do with them. As Lucy Jane and Marie had not reached their *pas de deux*, they were still uneasy and exchanged anxious glances.

"I hope we get to the *pas de deux* next time," Lucy Jane whispered to Marie, who was looking very pale and nervous.

"I hope we get it over and can go home," Marie replied, fiddling with her white blouse and flowered headdress. "These Russian peasant clothes are so hot. I'll be glad when we do the *Moon Ballet*," she said. "I don't like this one so

much. But I love the chiffon dresses and pale leotard and tights for the Moon Ballet."

"Let's think about this dance now," Lucy Jane said, concerned that Marie would mess up their *pas de deux* if she wasn't concentrating.

Once the director was in the recording van and could see the children on camera, he asked them to start again. This time they got to the end of the dance, but made more mistakes than they had ever made before.

Miss Marova looked very disappointed. Lucy Jane and Marie stood shamefaced. Two boys had fallen over as they did their kicks. They had to kick their legs forward while crouched and almost sitting on their heels. They swore in Russian and Miss Marova looked even more cross and shook her finger at them.

"Places," the first assistant director said in Russian, listening to his earphones and repeating the director's instructions. "If we have to stop please keep your places until we start filming again."

Miss Marova repeated his instructions, and the children ran to their starting positions. Miss Marova walked to the centre of the studio, stood there a moment looking at the children, and then suddenly blew them kisses and made a gesture of support. The children responded with a thumbs-up sign and the music began.

The cameras recorded the dance from three different positions. One cameraman was on a crane and could move up and down, so he could film the children from above or below. A second cameraman was static at the far end of the studio, where he could see everyone in long shot, and the third cameraman had a portable camera on his shoulder and from time to time followed the children around, which was very disconcerting as he was often in the way.

Lucy Jane was determined not to let anything distract her, so she continued to dance her heart out.

Downstairs in the recording caravan the director sat with the principal of the school. Madame Krotchenova sat intently watching the scenes, her hunched body like a black insect peering at the young dancers on the screen. When the children had got to the end of their dance she turned to the director and said in Russian, "Put the camera on this girl," and she pointed to a little figure on the side of the scene. It was Lucy Jane. "Please, I would like the camera to follow her, I want to watch her more closely."

The second time they recorded the dance, one camera was trained in on Lucy Jane. Luckily Lucy Jane wasn't aware of this and continued to dance her best. When the recording was finished the principal said, "Please show me more of this girl when they do the next dance." The director agreed.

Upstairs in the studio Miss Marova congratulated the children on their performance, and said, "There is only one bit the director needs to do again, that is Marie and Lucy Jane's *pas de deux*. This is not because the girls have gone wrong, but the cameraman, who was walking between the dancers to film them, was seen in the shot."

So the girls repeated their *pas de deux*. This time they danced

with even more sparkle and energy than they had before. Lucy Jane felt as if her soul was taking flight. Her face glowed with the inner happiness that came with dancing well. When they had finished Miss Marova was so pleased with them that she wanted to hug them. But she just smiled and blew them a kiss.

When the children had finished filming the folk dance, they had lunch, then they changed into their next costumes. When they were ready they went to another studio, which was converted into a small theatre, to film the *Moon Ballet*. The costumes for this ballet, which Miss Marova had choreographed herself, made the children look so delicate they could be blown away. The floating, multicoloured pastel chiffon leotards and tights suited all the girls beautifully. The girls wore their hair loose, and it flowed down their backs when they danced, making them look exceptionally ethereal and pretty.

The *Moon Ballet* was much more demanding and technically difficult, so the children dipped their shoes into the rosin box and rubbed and crushed the rosin under their feet so they would not slip. As they waited they practised the steps or warmed up, doing *pliés*, *battements tendus*, *grands battements* and *jetés*. They still wore their leg warmers until the last minute, although it was a hot day, as the children found it easier to dance when their muscles were warm. Once the lights were in position and turned on, it became unbearably hot, too hot, and the children were relieved they were in flimsy costumes.

As Lucy Jane danced the *Moon Ballet*, she really felt she was a ballerina. The classical ballet movements and music made her feel as if she was living in another world. Once again they rehearsed for the cameras and again Miss Marova gave them encouragement.

As they danced, their feet not making a sound, their bodies graceful and perfect, Miss Marova looked on happily.

Meanwhile the principal was still downstairs in the caravan watching the children rehearse on camera. "Let me see this girl again," and she pointed once more to Lucy Jane.

The director gave instructions for the cameraman to show Lucy Jane as she danced. Then Madame Krotchenova said, "Show me the girl's feet. Put the camera on to her feet and legs. I have seen the facial expressions and body." So the camera trained in on Lucy Jane's legs and feet. The principal said nothing, but after a time she demanded, "Get me Tatiana. I want to talk to her."

The director, who was annoyed at all the interruptions, sent a message down to the studio to fetch Miss Marova. A few minutes later, a very worried-looking Tatiana Marova arrived out of breath in the video caravan. "What is it?" she asked the principal.

Madame Krotchenova looked at her. "Why didn't you tell me about this little one?" she said, pointing to Lucy Jane. "And this one." She then pointed to Marie.

"I'm not sure what you mean," Miss Marova replied nervously.

"I mean, these girls could be as good as our girls. These

girls dance like a good Russian dancer. Why don't they have a solo?" she finished.

"Well," Miss Marova started slowly in Russian. "It's only this last week that they have really become so good, and then it was too late."

"I see. I must see these girls," the principal insisted. "Send them to me after the recording."

"Yes," Miss Marova said, thrilled that the principal of the Hirkov Ballet School, who was famous for being so difficult to please, liked Miss Marova's two young star dancers. Hadn't she once called Lucy Jane a little star? Lucy Jane had proved her right.

When the recording was over and Lucy Jane and Marie hadn't any more to do, Miss Marova came to them and said, "The principal would like to see you in the little studio on the ground floor."

Lucy Jane looked anxiously at Miss Marova, and asked, "Why?"

"Just go," Miss Marova said, and left the two girls to change and worry about what was to come. Then they hurried along to the studio, as quickly as they could, their hearts pounding.

The principal was at the far side of the studio, practising a little movement in front of the mirror. The girls stood before her silently, too frightened to speak. the principal looked at them. "Take off your skirts," she said to the girls. Lucy Jane and Marie took off their skirts and stood in their white pants and T-shirts which came down to the top of their thighs. "Please go the *barre*," the principal demanded. The two girls obeyed. The principal asked them to do their exercises without their ballet shoes. As they danced she said nothing, just looked fierce and did not give the girls a word of encouragement. After fifteen minutes both Lucy Jane and Marie were sweating and exhausted from the tension, and their muscles were shaking from tiredness. They had worked hard since early morning and it had been an extraordinarily taxing day.

At last Madame Krotchenova said, "I like your dancing very much. You can be good ballerinas. What is your name?" she asked Lucy Jane.

"Lucy Jane Tadworth," Lucy Jane replied quietly.

"I train you at this school next summer," the principal said. "No fee," she continued, smiling, "just come for six weeks next year to study dance."

Lucy Jane could hardly believe her ears. The fact that the principal liked her dancing and thought she was good, was better than any of her dreams.

The principal asked, "Your name?" looking at Marie. "You are good too," she said. Marie was pleased but the full impact of the wonderful news hadn't really time to sink in, before Madame Krotchenova said, "And you will train also." Marie gave Lucy Jane a quick glance, both girls' eyes sparkled with amazement and delight.

"Go now," the principal ordered, before the girls had time to speak.

Lucy Jane and Marie said a nervous, "Thank you, good-bye, Madame," and scurried from the room, bursting with excitement, longing to tell their parents the wonderful news. They rushed to the telephone.

As luck would have it the telephone was free and Lucy Jane managed to get straight through to her mother for the first time ever. "I can come back here again for no money," she told her mother. "The principal liked the way I dance, Miss Sonia will be amazed, and—" Before she could finish there was a great noise in the corridor and Annette was shouting.

"Come on, quickly, they're showing us the recording in the big studio now!"

Lucy Jane blew a kiss to her mother down the phone. "Got to go, Mummy – I miss you, see you soon."

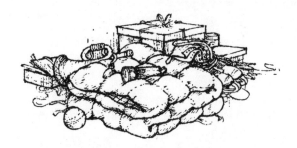

UGLY FEET ARE BEAUTIFUL

JAMES DAVID LANDIS

from The Sisters Impossible

Lily's haughty older sister Saundra is very good at ballet, and she's cross when Lily starts lessons too. But things get even worse when Saundra sees Lily talking to Meredith Meredith, her arch rival for a place in the school's company.

"CAN I TALK TO YOU, Saundra?"

"No."

"Please let me talk to you."

"No."

"I have to talk to you."

"No."

"Will you just listen if I talk?"

"No."

"Please."

"No."

"But I want to tell you—"

"Go to sleep, Lily."

"Saundra, please. Just for a few minutes."

"Go to sleep."

"I can't. I can't sleep."

"That's your tough luck."

69

"I won't be able to sleep until I can talk to you."

"No. Now shut up. I'm going to sleep. I have a very hard class tomorrow."

"You do? Tell me about it."

"There's nothing to tell."

"What's so hard about it?"

"Nothing in particular. It's just hard, that's all."

"It's always hard, I guess. Is it always hard, Saundra?"

"Yes, it's always hard."

"But it's worth it, isn't it? It always feels good after, doesn't it?"

"It feels terrible sometimes."

"What do you mean? Like you're stiff and your feet hurt?"

"That too, but –"

"I was stiff just today! I know exactly what you mean."

"It hurts more in your mind."

"What do you mean?"

"It hurts more to know that you were crappy."

"Crappy?"

"That you danced terribly today, that you danced terribly yesterday, and that you'll probably dance terribly tomorrow."

"Then why do you do it?"

"Because sometimes you think that tomorrow, tomorrow you'll dance beautifully."

"Maybe you will."

"Yes. Maybe I will. Now, go to sleep, Lily."

"But I have to talk to you."

"I have nothing to say to you. Not after what you did to me today."

"But what did I do?"

"I don't want to go into it again."

"But you never did go into it."

"And I'm not going into it now."

"Please. Just a short discussion."

"No."

"OK. Can I ask you a question? About something else, I mean?"

"What?"

"How come you don't chew gum?"

"What kind of question is that?"

"I noticed that almost everyone else at dancing school – or at least all the older girls – they all chew gum. But you don't."

"I guess I don't."

"How come? Because it looks so vulgar?"

"Where did you learn that word?"

"From Mom. So is that why you don't chew gum? Because it's vulgar?"

"No."

"Because you don't like the taste, then?"

"I like the taste all right."

"Then why don't you chew gum?"

"I don't like what it does to the shape of my jaw."

"You have a great jaw. I wish *I* had a jaw like yours. Your jaw is so haughty."

"Where did you learn that word? As if I have to ask."

"Mom again."

"So I have a haughty jaw, huh?"

"You know what I mean. But what does chewing gum have to do with it?"

"It changes the shape of your jaw."

"It does?"

"Certainly. Think of how many times you chew a single piece of gum. Then think of how many pieces of gum you would chew in a day. Then think of how many days you chew gum in a year. Then multiply."

"I can't. Not in my head, anyway."

"I didn't mean for you to do the arithmetic. I just meant for you to think of what so much chewing would do to your jaw."

"Oh. Then how come all the other girls chew gum all the time?"

"They're nervous."

"Are you nervous?"

"Sometimes."

"So how come you don't chew gum?"

71

"I told you. I don't like what it does to the shape of my jaw."

"But what does it do exactly?"

"It lowers it."

"It lowers what?"

"My jaw, stupid."

"You mean, it makes it less haughty."

"If you want to put it that way."

"Why do you want a haughty jaw anyway?"

"Why do *you* want one?"

"Me?"

"Yes. You said you want a jaw like mine. Just a minute ago."

"Gee. I guess you're right."

"But then, Lily, you're not a person who remembers anything she says."

"I do too."

"What about our *deal*, Lily?"

"We don't have a deal."

"Oh yes we do. You were supposed to tell Mom and Dad that you hated dancing school and you never wanted to go back again."

"But I didn't hate it."

"But you *though*t you would."

"I know it."

"And you were supposed to tell them that you did."

"No I wasn't. And I didn't."

"I know you didn't."

"I mean I didn't hate it."

"And I mean you didn't tell them."

"I told them the truth."

"Then you lied to me."

"No I didn't."

"Yes you did. We had a deal."

"I never said we did."

"We had a deal, Lily. That's all there is to it. We had a deal, and you're breaking our deal. It's the last deal we're ever going to have."

"But we *didn't. You* said we had a deal. *I* never said we did."

"Go to sleep. I don't want to talk about it anymore. It's making me angry, and if I get angry, I won't be able to sleep. And I don't even want to think about how you were talking to Meredith Meredith. Go to sleep. Leave me alone."

"I can't go to sleep."

"That's your problem."

"But I wasn't talking to Meredith Meredith. I mean – I was talking to her, but it wasn't what you think. Saundra? Are you listening? Saundra. Talk to me. I need to talk to you. Saundra? Saundra?"

Soon Lily could hear Saundra breathing deeply. She knew her sister was asleep and that she couldn't talk to her any longer. But she still had so much to say. All the words were running through her mind. She could speak them and hear them inside her head. And they kept her awake.

They were words about their deal that wasn't a deal. They were words about Meredith Meredith and what Lily had really said to her. They were words that were questions about dancing. They were words that said, "Why don't you like me, Saundra? I'm your sister. Why don't you like me?" They were words from Lily to comfort Saundra, words to tell her that she was a terrific dancer and she would get the place in the company of the American Ballet Center and Lily would come to see her dance in the theatre and would shower applause on her until her hands hurt as much as Saundra's feet hurt.

So many words. And all so silent. Saundra didn't hear one of them. They all remained shut up in Lily's head. Pounding and pleading. They kept her awake for hours. She felt as if she had electricity on her skin. And a radio inside her head.

She tried to make herself go to sleep by thinking of dancing. She pictured herself in class, assuming first position, second position, all the positions, getting better with each one while the rest of the class went on struggling to keep their balance and not look foolish. Then she saw Miss Witt get up from her stool and come over to her and say, "You're really very good, Curly. What else can you do?" And at that, Lily let go of the *barre*, pranced across the room, leaped into the air, leaped again, fluttered through space, turned, twirled, turned, twirled, ran on her toes from one side of the room to the other, flew like a bird through the air. But as she saw herself do this in her mind, she saw that she looked more like Saundra than herself. And she realized that she, Lily, couldn't do any of this, and that Saundra – Saundra, who was fast asleep just across the room – could do it all. For Saundra it wasn't a dream. Saundra was a dancer.

Lily wondered what it felt like to dance. She knew she herself was just at the beginning. She had had only one lesson, after all. One lesson! That was nothing. But Saundra had been dancing almost every day for almost six years. Day after day, Saundra had packed her leotard and tights and shoes in her bag and had gone off to class. Before today, Lily hadn't had even an idea of what a dancing class looked like. The big room. The *barre* on one side. The mirror on the other. The piano player, who hadn't even been given a chance to play and spent the whole class slurping his coffee and reading his magazine.

Almost every day of her life for the past six years, Saundra

74

had been going off to such a room. It amazed Lily to think that one day, almost six years ago, Saundra had been the same age as Lily was now and had gone off to her very first class, just as Lily had today. Lily wondered if Saundra, too, had hated the idea of going to class before she ever went to one, and then, after her first class, had decided that she loved to dance. Lily wondered if Saundra's legs had gotten stiff after her first class.

It was impossible to sleep. There was so much to think about.

Lily threw off her thin summer blanket and sat up in bed. In the light from the streetlamp she could see clearly her feet sticking out from the bottom of her nightgown. Across the room Saundra was visible too, sleeping on her back, not covered by a blanket or even a sheet, her body stretched out, one leg straight, the other curled up in an L shape so that one foot rested on the other knee. It was as if Saundra, even sleeping, was dancing too. Lily could not deny it. Saundra was very beautiful and very graceful.

But what about her feet? Was it true, as her father had told her, that all dancers had ugly feet? And what had Saundra meant when she told Lily in the dressing room, "Worry about your feet," and had pointed to the girl next to her, the girl with the bloody feet? What about Saundra? What about Saundra's feet?

Lily slowly got up from the bed and walked as quietly as possible over to Saundra. She knelt down by Saundra's feet and looked at them, first at the one towards the bottom of the bed, then at the one that was resting on the other knee.

They looked perfectly fine to her. But the light in the room – the light from the streetlamp, for there was no moon – wasn't strong enough for close inspection of anything.

So Lily rose, being careful not to lean on Saundra's bed or to make any noise, and went to her closet. There – packed in with her sleeping bag and ice skates and the old bugle her father had given her but on which she'd never learned to play a single note or even to blow a single sound – was her flashlight. Because Saundra had never wanted a nightlight on in the room, Lily used to keep the flashlight next to her bed when she was younger and frightened of the dark. But now she hardly ever used it.

Lily tested the flashlight in the closet. It gave off a dim light. She went back to Saundra's bed and shone the flashlight on her sister's foot that was closest to the end of the bed.

Lily stared at each toe. Then she shook her head. It was hard to believe.

She shone the flashlight on the other foot. The toes were the same. But on this foot she could also see the bottom. She shook her head again and leaned closer to get an even better look.

It was unbelievable.

Almost every one of Saundra's toenails was black. One of the toenails was missing completely. Another one was separated from the toe and just kind of hanging there, ready to fall off.

The bottoms of her feet were all scaly, covered with thick skin that looked hard and shiny and rough.

Lily was fascinated. She couldn't take her eyes off Saundra's feet. They were kind of sickening. But at the same time, they were kind of beautiful. There was no question that her feet were ugly. But they were also beautiful.

"What are you looking at?"

Saundra's voice, in the dimly lit room, breaking into her concentration on Saundra's feet, almost made Lily jump. As it was, she dropped the flashlight, which landed on Saundra's shin.

"Ouch!" said Saundra.

"Sorry," said Lily meekly.

"What are you *doing*?"

"I lost something," Lily said.

"What?"

"I said, I lost something."

"No. I mean, *what* did you lose?"

Lily thought for a moment. It was no good to lie. "Nothing," she said.

"Did you or didn't you lose something?"

"No."

"You didn't?"

"No."

"Then what were you doing?"

"Looking at your feet."

"You were looking at my feet!" Saundra sounded really upset.

"Yes."

"That's an invasion of my privacy."

"I'm sorry," Lily apologized.

"Why were you looking at my feet?"

"I wanted to see them."

"In the middle of the night?"

"Well," said Lily, "you always keep them covered up in the daytime."

"I know I do. Did it ever occur to you why?"

77

"No."

"Well, now that you've seen them, Lily – *now* do you know why I keep them covered up?"

"I guess," said Lily.

"Why?" Saundra asked again.

Lily said nothing.

"I'll tell you why," said Saundra. "I'll show you why." She picked up the flashlight and shone it on her right foot. "Look at it," she ordered. "Look at it."

Lily looked.

"Take a good look," said Saundra.

Lily took a long look.

"That's why I hide them. Because they look like that."

Lily realized that Saundra had begun to cry.

"What's the matter?" she asked.

"Oh, nothing!" said Saundra, sniffling, obviously trying to make her tears go away by speaking gruffly.

"But they're beautiful," said Lily.

Saundra actually broke into laughter, even though she was still crying. "Oh, Lily," she said. "They're ugly. They're not beautiful. They're ugly. But that's not what's the matter. All dancers' feet are ugly. Mine are too. There's nothing you can do about it."

"So why are you crying?" asked Lily.

"I'm crying because I don't know if it's worth it."

"What do you mean?"

"I don't care if I have the ugliest feet in the world," said Saundra, "if I can be a great dancer. But what if I can't?"

"You already are."

Saundra stopped crying. She shook her head. "What if I can't?" she asked again. "Then what? Then it's not worth it. It's not worth having feet like this. It's not worth hurting your body. It's not worth spending almost every waking minute practising and studying and not thinking about anything else or doing anything else. It's not worth thinking that you're committing a sin against your body every time you eat an ice-cream cone. It's not worth it."

78

"I think it is," said Lily.

"How can you say that? What do you know about it? You've taken only one class, Lily. What can you possibly know about it?"

"I just think it's worth it," Lily said.

"But why?"

"It would be worth it to me if I could dance like you."

"You really think so?"

"Yes. And I think your feet are beautiful. I think you have beautiful feet."

"You must be blind."

"To me they're beautiful."

"Go to bed, Lily. It's the middle of the night. And you don't know what you're talking about. Go to bed."

Lily got up off her knees and walked back to her bed. As she covered herself with her thin blanket, she realized she hadn't seen or heard Saundra cry in years. It made her feel funny. It made her feel that her sister was even more beautiful than before, but less haughty. She wished she could help Saundra so she wouldn't cry anymore. Or else, so she would cry whenever she wanted to. Maybe Saundra was afraid. Maybe Saundra, deep down inside, was scared of dancing. Maybe she was scared of not dancing well enough to beat out Meredith Meredith for the place in the company. Maybe she was scared of being just an ordinary person who would never get up on a stage and have people applaud her until their hands ached and her own ears tingled with excitement.

To Lily, Saundra was not an ordinary person. But maybe to herself she was. It was hard to believe. But maybe she was, and all her haughty looks and her dancer's proud walk just hid what she felt inside: that she was an ordinary person.

"Good night, Saundra," Lily whispered across the room.

There was no answer.

"You're a special person," Lily said softly.

She listened hard for a response. All she finally heard, before she drifted off to sleep, was the sound of quiet crying.

SUMMER CAMP

CYNTHIA VOIGT

from Come a Stranger

MINA'S HEART WAS beating so fast, and so hard, she thought for sure it must show, thumping away under her blouse. Her father was driving slowly through the city of New London and then, slowly, up the river road. They had been riding for hours, without talking much, and Mina had made herself be patient. But now they were so close, and the car was going so slowly, waiting to turn and enter between the stone pillars and creeping up the road to the quadrangle.

When the car finally stopped, Mina burst out and took her suitcase from the back seat. Her father greeted Miss Maddinton. They talked about nothing in particular. Mina looked at her sneakers and felt her heart, beating.

It all soaked into her skin, and that was enough for now. If she looked around, at the stone buildings and trees, at all the familiar remembered places, she would start running around to touch everything, and her father would know – he'd know for sure what he'd only guessed, that she was gladder to be back at camp than anywhere else, that she could barely wait for him to leave so she could be by herself and be her own self again. She didn't want to hurt her father's feelings by letting him know that, so she stood there with her eyes closed, being there.

At last, he started to leave. "Have a good time, Mina." He hugged her close and she hugged him back, her head almost up to his shoulders now. "Behave yourself."

"I will. Have a good summer, Dad."

She made herself stand and wave while the car drove away, a dusty black sedan with the Maryland licence plate a little white square. Then she turned slowly around, and smiled.

"You're in room three-o-seven," Miss Maddinton said to her, consulting a list she had on her clipboard. She was wearing a silvery grey suit; her hair was in dark braids that she'd wound around her head like a corona. She looked busy, she looked distant and calm, she looked beautiful.

Mina was back where there was music around everywhere, every day. She was back where if you said Prokofiev, nobody said, "Who?"

"You've grown," Miss Maddinton said, sounding doubtful, looking doubtful.

What did she expect Mina to do? Not grow? Mina laughed out loud. "I guess. My mom says I've been shooting up and shooting out."

"You can find your own way, can't you? I've got to greet the new girls."

"Three-o-seven?" Mina asked, not that she didn't remember, but just to savour this first minute a little longer. "Is Tansy here yet?"

"She's up there," Miss Maddinton said.

At that, Mina couldn't wait another minute. She grabbed her suitcase and hurrying as fast as she could with the heavy case banging against her leg went into the dormitory, went home.

Room 307 was on the third floor. The second floor was for the littlest girls, the top floor for the fourteen year olds. Mina climbed two flights of stairs and pushed through the heavy door on to the corridor. She heard voices, she heard music.

Looking at the numbers painted on the doors, she went on down the hall. Her feet wanted to jump and run, her heart wanted to stop it all from going by so fast already. Room 307 was down towards the far end of the corridor. Mina guessed Tansy was probably in somebody else's room, visiting.

But the room only had one bed in it. The room was too small for two beds anyway. The room was a single room.

Mina put her suitcase down on the floor and sat down on the bed. For a long minute her mind was empty – blank and silent, a cold white emptiness. Then she understood.

They were seeing the outside of her.

Because nobody, not even Tansy, had wanted to be her roommate. So the adults had put her in a single room too.

Mina got up and set her suitcase on the bed. She unpacked her clothes into the dresser, then made up the bed and thought. She just hadn't understood, she guessed; but as soon as she thought that she knew she was wrong. They *had* all been friends, they had all got along just fine. It was what her father had said, though, what he had noticed right away when he picked her up: she was the only little black girl there.

Mina laughed out loud and dropped the pillow on the bed. Little? Well, she wasn't any too little anymore. There were bras and a box of Kotex she'd unpacked with the rest of her things. She guessed, if they thought she was little, in any way, they were underestimating her. She guessed she was going to have to make friends with them all over again. She stretched her arms out, her broad shoulders up, and flexed her fingers. She didn't mind that. She always liked making friends.

The first thing she wanted to do, now, had changed. Now the first thing she wanted to do was go outside and wander around a little. She wanted to have her bare feet on the grass that covered these hills. She wanted to put her palms up against the bark of the trees, to feel how strong and solid the trees were. She wanted to hear the way the wind blew through leafy branches, and she wanted to put her eyes once again on the grey stone buildings that looked like they had grown up out of the earth to make the college. Once she had touched all of those things, once she'd got back in touch with those things that didn't look at her and see just the outside, Mina would come back inside and start dealing with the human beings.

When Mina found Tansy, it was in a room with Isadora. They were sitting on their beds, not talking, not playing Tansy's music, not doing anything. Tansy looked like her same mousy self. Isadora had grown up. You could see what she would look like when she finished growing, Mina thought; Isadora looked like a dancer.

Mina smiled and sat down and pretended she didn't notice the quick, worried glance Isadora sent Tansy. Last year, when she had been asleep to what was really going, on, Mina had mostly caught only the ends of those looks and been puzzled. Now that she was awake, she could see what they were. They separated her from everybody else, from everybody white. She thought she could show them that wasn't necessary.

"Hey, hi. It's good to see you." Because it was. "Isn't it fun to be back? Have you seen Charlie?"

Isadora knew the answer to that. "She's going to a drama camp, instead. Near Philadelphia. She said she's got all ballet has to offer her."

"Oh-ho," Mina guessed without stopping to think, "and I bet we call her Charlotte from here on."

Isadora looked up at her and laughed. "How'd you know? Honestly, Mina you wouldn't have believed it. She came, Charlotte, to spend the night, sometime in April. We'd planned it for ages, and then all she could talk about was this camp, and the opportunities it offered. She was like – she was like she was twenty-two and talking about her career. The first thing she said to me was exactly that: I had to call her Charlotte. How'd you know?"

"It was a guess." Mina smiled another hello at Tansy, noticing for the first time what a shy smile Tansy had. Her mouth barely moved.

"And she was wearing stockings and three-inch heels to come spend the night."

"You've got braces," Mina said to Tansy, whose mouth was filled with silver metal. "Do they hurt?"

"A little."

"I liked your Christmas card." It had a picture of Tansy's whole family on it, dressed up, standing in front of a big fireplace. Rich folks, Zandor had commented. "Your mother's pretty."

Tansy nodded.

"Have you made up any new dances?" Mina asked her. That got Tansy going, and Isadora drifted out of the room saying she'd be back to go down to dinner with them, so they should be sure to wait.

It didn't take Mina long to figure it out. They didn't mind being friends with her, but they didn't want to be roommates. They thought she wouldn't notice, as if she could be smart about other things but not about this. It was pretty funny, when she thought about it. Most of the time it was funny, she admitted to herself, alone in her room at night, sometimes, especially alone in her room, it felt like teeth biting into her heart. Like sharp pointed teeth biting into where her feelings were and cutting off bites to chew on. "But what did you think?" she asked herself at such times. "Didn't you know you were black?"

She wasn't going to let it trouble her.

What did trouble her was that for some reason the classes weren't going right. Mina had worked hard to maintain her dance, harder than she'd ever worked at anything. But she seemed to have fallen behind even so. What used to be easy was hard now, as if she couldn't do things everybody else could. Or as if her body couldn't do what she wanted it to. When they had their dance classes, Mina would be distracted by the mirrors, because they reflected her blackness back and back, among the white skin of the other girls. That was the hardest place, the dance class, to remember not to see just the outside of herself, not to notice how different she was from everybody else. The other girls sat out in the sun to get tan, Mina thought; but she was darker than any of them, and it was funny that they didn't see how funny it was. Mina felt trapped in her skin, locked in it, like a jail. She was always aware of being the only one.

Miss Maddinton didn't seem to think anything was wrong, even when Mina found herself sweating after doing what should be simple floor exercises. Miss Maddinton never had any complaints abut Mina. So Mina figured whatever felt so wrong was all in her own head. The theory class was still terrific, listening to different composers, learning about harmonics, watching Mr Tattodine bounce around getting all excited about the music.

The first week of camp lasted about a hundred years. Mina never could relax, unless she was alone outside. Alone inside, she had to keep pushing back thoughts she didn't want to face. With other people, she felt confused, trying to figure out what really was going on. They liked her, the other girls; they didn't mind sitting with her at the table or anything like that, and they included her in the things they did, and they laughed when she was silly and listened to what she had to say. They talked to her. But Mina couldn't tell if it was her,

Mina, inside her skin, they liked, or if they were being nice to the one black girl at camp. If you were walking down a street and you saw somebody all crippled up and walking peculiarly, you'd go out of your way to show that it didn't make any difference, to act natural and friendly, to smile and all that. You'd do it because you didn't want the person to think you were thinking what you were thinking.

When they talked, nobody asked her questions. She asked them questions and they answered, as if they were the interesting ones and it was only natural that she should want to know more about them and that they shouldn't be interested in knowing anything about her. So Mina was always listening to what was being talked about, trying to figure out what it really meant. There were also some things that never got mentioned, as if they weren't visible. Like anything to do with black skin.

What did it mean? When the questions crowded into her mind too closely, Mina would go outside, alone. She would sit back against a tree and close her eyes. She could feel the tree behind her, connected to its roots under the earth and growing straight up into the sky, strong. She could feel the ground under her legs, the grass-growing soil that covered the rocks that shaped the hills. Neither the trees nor the earth had any eyes to see what colour she was.

In Narnia, Mina would want to be a dryad, a tree creature, with her roots dug into the earth and her body strong and lasting, untroubled by questions that blew through her like a wind blowing through branches. Trees were peaceful. They knew what was really true.

As soon as Mina thought that, however, and just when a smile was starting up in her heart and her whole body was relaxing against the grass and the tree, she would remember dryads came from Greek mythology. They belonged to the white world. Then she would have to jump up with the feeling that jumped up inside her. Because they had so much, they had everything, and they kept reminding her that it wasn't any of it hers.

Mina was so tired at the end of that first week of camp she didn't think she'd ever make it through without the company of the trees. The trees were stronger and older, wiser and truer too.

The second week was just about as bad. Mina was at ease only when she was alone, or during Mr Tattodine's class listening to music. She thought about how many of the instruments were made out of wood – violins and piano, cello, and the reeds, the oboe, the clarinet, the resonating bassoon. She picked out their individual voices as she listened. The Fourth of July came at the end of the second week. The girls at the camp had been invited to a big bicentennial display of fireworks over at the naval base across the river, so after supper that night they went to get dressed for the occasion. Mina, alone in her room, used the blow drier to make her shoulder length hair into a smooth pageboy. She got a little too much of the straightening gel into it, so it looked as if it had been lacquered into place, not soft the way it was supposed to. She didn't have time to wash it out and redo it. She put on the dress Eleanor had made from a pattern Mina sent. It was a pale blue dress, with a sleeveless blouse top over an A-line skirt. Mina checked herself in the mirror, letting the noises from the other rooms slide in and out of her ears. Then she went to the window.

The sun was low in the sky, a heavy summer sun, sinking. There was no wind for a change, and the air lay heavy and gold. The trees stood patiently, enduring.

Mina closed her eyes. She wanted to be back with her own family, with her own people, at the annual Fourth of July church picnic. They didn't have fireworks, except for a few sparklers for the little children, but they had fried chicken and potato salad and singing. There were three or four churches that got together for the occasion, a big, noisy crowd of people. The stars were fireworks enough, Mina didn't think fireworks were so special. Right now, she could almost see long tables set out, covered with food, and hear the people talking. She wished she was there where she wasn't pretending every waking hour not to be different, pretending she was something she wasn't, acting as if she wanted to be white.

Mina's eyes flew open. They were making her act as if she was white, or as if she wished she was.

"Who's making you do that, Missy?" she asked herself. She asked it out loud, but answered it silently: I am, or I'm letting them, which is about the same thing. And she was ashamed of herself. Angry too.

No more, she promised herself. She was going to be herself, Mina Smiths, t-roub-le. She felt the devilment rising up in her.

Mina went right out to the big seat that ran across the rear of the school bus. That way, there was room for anybody who wanted to sit with her, but nobody who didn't want to would have to. Tansy and Isadora and Natalie came to the back to join her. They watched people get into the bus. The oldest girls were dressed up pretty fine, Mina noticed, with as much eyeshadow as they thought they could get away with. "Because of the sailors over there," Isadora explained.

Isadora had mascara on, Mina saw, and lipstick. "You're doing it too – don't try to kid me."

"Don't be—" Isadora started to say, then she saw something on Mina's face that made her giggle instead. "They're awfully cute in those uniforms. You're just jealous."

"Don't you wish," Mina said, and the girls around them said, "That's telling her." But Mina looked around her, at the heads of hair that shone silky clean in so many colours, and at the slender necks that looked delicate even though they were, she knew, strong. She looked strong, she knew that, big and strong. And she was too.

"We'll have to get you introduced to one of them," she said to Isadora. "Maybe you should fall into the river."

"I can swim."

"You can pretend, can't you? Splash around and yell for help. Then he comes to rescue you."

Many faces were turned around to watch this conversation.

"I couldn't do that," Isadora said.

"OK, then I'll push you."

Miss Maddinton told them to be quiet, to behave with some dignity please, and the bus started up.

As the sun went down, they watched the flag being lowered, while a bugle blew taps. Everybody stood quiet to watch, listening to the sad, lonely notes of the bugle. Four marines stood at attention, while two others lowered the flag and folded it. Mina looked around at the crowd: officers and their families, lots of children standing quiet, sailors in bright white uniforms, and civilian groups. Except for a couple of the marines, she was the only black person there. She felt as if everybody must be noticing her, standing there among the girls from the camp.

She wasn't going to let that get her down. When they sang *The Star-Spangled Banner* to music from the loudspeaker, Mina just went ahead and sang out. All around her, quiet white voices sang in a reined-in way, fading away on the high notes. Not Mina; Mina sang strong and true, letting her voice dominate. Let people notice her, if they wanted to.

"You have a nice voice," Tansy whispered as they sat down, getting ready to watch the fireworks.

"You bet," Mina said. She heard people chuckling at her reply, because what they would have said was something modest, like, "Oh, do you think so?" or "Not really, I just like singing the anthem."

While they waited, the last light faded out of the sky, and a little breeze came up along the river. They were sitting fairly far back from the river's edge, all of the dance camp girls together, supervised by the teachers. Mina wanted to sit closer to the water, because that would be a better view. She whispered to Isadora, asking if she wanted to move up.

"We have to stay here."

"Nobody'll know, nobody'll see us, because it's dark."

Isadora's shadowed face looked around. She got up, while Mina told Tansy, who didn't want to come with them. Mina and Isadora moved along the edge of their group, like shadows, Mina thought.

But not enough like shadows to escape Miss Maddinton. "Isadora?" she called. "Where do you think you're off to?"

She said it as if it was Isadora's idea, as if Mina was just following Isadora. It was as if she wasn't going to call out at Mina because then she would be picking on Mina because she was black. As if Mina was a mouse like Tansy and couldn't get herself into her own trouble. As if she got special treatment. All of this rushed through Mina's mind in a second and fed the devilment.

"We's gwine down to de lebee," Mina called out. "To pick us some wateymelon." She barely got the words out before she doubled over laughing. Everyone around started laughing too, and she and Isadora returned to their places. "Honestly, Mina," they said. "How could you?" they giggled.

A light exploded in the sky, a huge white light that plumed out like a chrysanthemum, and then two more exploded behind it. It knocked the breath out of Mina. When the three crackers went off, like cannon across the skies, she wanted to jump up and cry out something. *Whoo-ee*, that was what was in her mouth. The audience clapped, instead.

Mina just shook her head. If this was what a super big fireworks display was like, she guessed she could see why they thought it was such a big thing. She couldn't figure out why they just applauded it, like it was a theatre. She went along with them, patting her palms together, but that wasn't the way to do justice to what was going on in the sky overhead.

The sky filled, over and over again, with explosions of white and red and orange, with whirligigs that spun upwards and then showered down like falling stars. Mina watched with big eyes. The fireworks shone out against the sky. When they faded, the black sky waited there, pricked with stars, silent, until the next explosion of light and sound.

Finally, Mina couldn't hold it in, because she didn't want to. "Whoo-eee," she called out, like a trumpet, to the falling fires. All around, voices shushed her.

On Monday of the third week. Mr Tattodine came to their dance class with a video camera to record them. Miss Maddinton told them to ignore it, and after a few minutes they could. Mina found it easy to forget the white head with its eye fixed into the viewer of the black box. Mina was working hard, as usual. She wondered – while she concentrated on getting her legs right and her arms right, to keep her body in the balance Miss Maddinton showed them – if she was in some kind of transition stage in her dancing. She didn't remember that it used to be this much trouble. It used to be as natural as breathing. The class, warmed up now by the *barre* exercises, moved to the centre of the room. Mina continued to wonder.

If it was like – like being a seed in your seed case; there would come a time when you had to break out of the case and force your roots through. Or like being pregnant, and then the labour of having your baby; it was easy to get pregnant, and her mother always talked about how good her body felt when she was carrying her children, close inside her. But before the baby could have its own life, it and the mother had to work it out. The class did the *port de bras* movement, while the piano played a theme from *Swan Lake*. And Mina wondered, feeling how her muscles seemed to pull at her shoulder bones, feeling big and clumsy among the swaying torsos.

Belle and she had once watched a crab go through the final stages of shedding its old shell. They had found it hidden among the grass at the edge of a creek. Crabs shed their old shells when they got too big for them, Mina had always known that. At the season of every full moon, people went looking among the shallow waters for the soft-shelled crabs, which could be fried up whole and eaten. Mina didn't care much for soft-shells, except for the crunchy thin legs. But after they had watched the crab pulling itself out of its outgrown undersized shell – after she had seen the contractions of muscles under the flesh as it patiently pulled each leg free, working backwards out of the old shell . . . it looked like someone with no fingers trying to take of his socks. It hurt Mina and made her impatient, watching it. She wanted the process to be over, even though she knew that the crab would be helpless for the next day or so while it grew its new shell. She knew that the other crabs, who weren't shedding, would come through the shallow waters, looking for dinner, as would the herons and egrets. The process of shedding was painful to watch – as the crab gathered its dwindling strength to pull its legs free and force itself backwards through a narrow crack in the hard old shell, achieving another quarter-inch of freedom – Mina ran away, that long ago summer day. This day, however, she wasn't going to run away. She thought something like shedding was happening to her. Miss Maddinton called out for the class to do *batterie en demi-pointe* and Mina pulled her muscles together to try it. It was not too successful, but she kept on trying and kept on smiling, kept pulling up into the air and beating with her foot. It almost always missed one beat, and she grinned, thinking of how it must look.

Miss Maddinton had a private conference with everyone in her class. She met with them in the dormitory living room.

First they watched the tape, then they talked about technique and poise and what needed improvement. Mina was one of the first, although not the very first. Sitting in the big armchair, watching the square screen, Mina saw more clearly than anytime before exactly how much she stood out. She tried to watch the whole class, or the whole performing group, but she kept seeing the one black person there. Miss Maddinton didn't say anything while they watched, except to hurry on past parts where Mina didn't appear. She didn't stop the tape to discuss any special problem.

Mina watched the big black girl on the screen. The girl looked clumsy. Not clumsy by ordinary standards, but clumsy in comparison to everyone else there dancing.

Then Miss Maddinton put in another tape: It was Mina's audition tape, a little black girl who wasn't too skilful, but danced easily, naturally, and with a pleasure that made you smile to see her.

After both tapes were finished Miss Maddinton sat back in her chair, her legs stretched out in front of her. Miss Maddinton always wore dancing slippers for shoes. "What do you think?" she asked Mina. "You see what I mean, don't you?"

"Do you think I'm more disciplined?" Mina asked. "I think I am." She was a little frightened, and she was afraid she knew why.

Miss Maddinton stood up. She went over to one of the long windows that looked on the trees and grass. She turned to face Mina.

"I don't know what to do about you." she said. "I don't know what's the right thing to do."

"What's the matter?" Mina asked.

"You saw it, I know you did. I guess I can't expect you to make it easy for me, after you've fought so hard to come this far. You've grown uncoordinated, Mina," she said. "You're too far behind the rest of the class, and falling farther behind every day. I think you know that."

No, Mina hadn't known that. She couldn't kid herself about

93

not seeing it when she watched the tape. But she hadn't thought that it was happening because she wasn't good enough. "It's not that bad," she said.

"I'm not saying it's your fault. There's nothing you can do about it. This just happens, with singers as well as dancers, at puberty. Nobody can really predict how a body will develop over the years of change. Your people develop earlier, which is why it's happened to you this year."

"It's because I'm black, isn't it?" Mina asked. Maybe the girls could avoid talking about it, but they were children and Miss Maddinton was a grown-up.

"That's ridiculous." Miss Maddinton sounded like she had known Mina was going to ask that.

"No," Mina said. "No, I don't think it is. You just said it was, in fact."

"What I just said, Mina, is that you're awkward and ungainly. That's what I meant and that's what I said. Although you don't see many black ballerinas—"

"And what about the Harlem Dance Theatre?" Mina demanded. If she'd talked like that at home, her mother would have stopped her mouth. But she wasn't at home.

"Not in the classical ballet," Miss Maddinton went on, as if she was thinking out loud. "I don't know . . . Next time I'm going to insist on at least two of you; you'd have felt better with someone like you here, wouldn't you? Or four, if we must have any, if we must have the federal funding. The trouble is, you're so mature. Not only physically, so it's hard to know – Georges Tattodine says you do well in theory, he says you've an excellent memory and a perfect ear and – but it's not fair to you, nor to our executive committee. It costs money, for room and board if nothing else."

"I could try harder," Mina said. She sat very still in her chair.

"You know as well as I do how hard you're trying right now. You have, as you rightly said, learned discipline."

"Then why don't you give me a chance?" Mina demanded. Miss Maddinton's eyes grew cold.

"Why do you think I've delayed making this decision? I thought this would happen, and I saw it right away, but I thought, maybe— Oh, I wanted to avoid trouble too."

"I'm not any trouble," Mina insisted. "I try. I practise. I'm more serious than a lot of them. You know that's true."

"But it's not getting any better, and it's certainly not getting any easier. It can't be a happy time for you," Miss Maddinton insisted.

"I'm not unhappy," Mina said.

"Because," Miss Maddinton went on, thinking correctly that Mina was trying to avoid the main point, "you're starting to clown around, to turn errors and clumsiness into a joke. Mina?"

"Yes, ma'am," Mina said, collapsing inside herself, like a tree finally felled. Miss Maddinton was right. But she didn't want to say so out loud. That was all Mina wanted now, just not to have to say so out loud, herself that she was no longer good enough.

"What do you think, Mina?" Miss Maddinton kept after her. For these conferences, she wore white slacks and a silvery pink, pale shirt. She stood in front of the window, not moving, and Mina knew that until she'd said what Miss Maddinton wanted to hear, the conversation wouldn't be over.

"I'm the worst in the class," Mina admitted.

Miss Maddinton waited. Mina felt helpless. She was helpless against Miss Maddinton's cold discipline, and she was about not to be able to control her tears any longer, so she was helpless against herself too.

"What do you want me to do?" Mina asked, almost pleading with Miss Maddinton, just to say something, make some decision and then make Mina obey, just to have this finished with.

"Mr Tattodine notwithstanding, you're going to have to go home."

"Go home? Why do I have to do that?"

Miss Maddinton sighed and shook her head at Mina's stupidity.

"I could drop the ballet class. I don't have to take that if you think I'm so bad. But I could still take theory and do the evening things. I don't want to go home."

"Pull yourself together, Mina. *Faites attention*. Oh, you get along with the girls. I'll admit that; I've been surprised at how successful that's been. You handle yourself with real maturity. But it won't do to have a girl here who isn't taking dance. You know that as well as I. We have neither staff nor courses to take that responsibility. It's always hard to admit that you've failed—"

At that, Mina was so angry that she did burst into tears. She was so angry she just wept. She was weeping so hard she couldn't speak. Just growing wasn't failure, you couldn't say someone had failed because her body grew bosoms and hips and the muscles worked differently.

"But, Mina, what do want me to say? What can I do? What do you want to do?"

"I want to go home," Mina wailed, miserable, angry, and ashamed.

"Good," Miss Maddinton said, ushering Mina out of the room now that Mina had said what she wanted to hear.

It was all settled by the next day. Most of the girls avoided Mina, as if she had some horrible contagious disease. "That's tough," Isadora said. "I'm glad I've still got a dancer's body. I'll keep it, my parents are both slight."

Tansy had been kinder. "I'll miss you, you make things more fun," Tansy said, her big brown mouse eyes showing that she meant it. For all the difference that made.

Mina didn't know what to say to anybody, so she didn't say anything. When Mr Tattodine put her on the morning train to go south, he told her to keep on studying music. "You've got real ability," he said, his face looking worried.

Mina just nodded. She shook the hand he held out for her to shake.

She sat by herself on the train, with her suitcase on the rack above her. There were several other people on the train and

Mina just kept looking out the window so that she wouldn't see them looking at her. Everything was quiet except for the train noises. The train went on south, stopping at places, New Haven and Bridgeport, Stamford, and then it went underground to get into New York. Mina sat still and waited. They'd given her some money for lunch, but she wasn't hungry. They'd told her that her family knew when she was getting into Wilmington and would meet her, but she didn't wonder about that, even though she remembered that her father had the car.

At New York, there were more people who got on the train, and the car started to fill up with music from radios, and with voices talking, and with little children. Mina stared out the window, seeing no difference between the dark tunnel of New York and the industrial towns of New Jersey and the rolling countryside past Philadelphia.

She didn't know what she was going to do, she couldn't think of anything she wanted to do. She knew the camp hadn't turned her out, not exactly, but she felt like they had.

She knew that they had turned her out because of the dancing, but she felt like they had done it because she was black. She was afraid they'd only let her come in the first place just because she was black.

A lot of people were getting off in Wilmington. Mina stepped off the air-conditioned train and into what felt like a solid wall of heat. She hesitated briefly, then moved away from the throngs, moving along the platform, looking up and down the platform.

It was hot on the asphalt and the air shimmered with heat and moisture. Her blouse stuck to her skin, but the air felt good as it wrapped around her body. She didn't mind nobody being right there, mostly because she didn't know what she'd say to Zandor or her mother. She guessed she might never say anything again because when she looked down her throat to find words, there weren't any there. She felt locked away into the silence she had been moving around in for the last twenty-four hours.

They sure got her out of there fast enough, once they got moving. As if they couldn't wait to get rid of her.

People moved away and the platform got empty. The sun poured down through the thick air. There was a city smell to the air, metal and engine fumes. City noises were moving, off in some distance. Mina stood. She wasn't waiting, because she didn't much look forward to being picked up. She didn't know what she was going to say to anybody, especially when she knew perfectly well that what she'd been thinking – for the last year and more – had been getting-away-from-them thoughts.

But she wanted to see her mother, she wanted Momma's arms and love wrapped around her. Her momma would be angry at the camp, she'd be all on Mina's side no matter what. Mina wanted some of the kind of love Momma gave to her children, where love was the first and deepest thing, and the questions came later and the answers wouldn't matter much measured up against the love.

But she didn't want to see her momma, because she didn't know what to say.

When a big man, dressed up fine in a dark suit and tie, his shoes polished to high gloss, came walking up towards her, Mina got ready to run if she had to. She'd leave her suitcase. It only had dance things in it anyway, and she wouldn't need those. She didn't know if she'd have to run, but she thought if he looked like he might grab for her she'd take off, go inside to the waiting room where there were people around. Just because someone was black didn't mean you could trust them.

"Wilhemina Smiths? I'm sorry to be late. I had trouble parking. I'm supposed to escort you home," his voice went on talking. Mina stared at him, not hearing what he was saying.

He looked vaguely familiar, with heavy straight eyebrows and round, sympathetic eyes, as he introduced himself and reached out to take her suitcase for her. Then she could identify him, although she'd missed his name. He was Alice's husband, the summer minister. She wondered if she was about to meet Alice, and she hoped so at the same time as she didn't want to. Not now, not like this.

She walked along beside the man. He tried asking her a couple of questions, how her trip was, whether she minded travelling alone. Mina just nodded or shook her head. She wondered why her mother hadn't come. She hoped her mother wasn't angry with her.

The summer minister had a big, dusty station wagon. He put Mina's suitcase in the back. The rear seat had two child car-seats strapped on it. He asked her if she wanted to sit in front or in back. Mina sat in the front seat. He told her to strap in, and Mina pulled the seatbelt down and latched it. He asked her to be sure she knew how to unlatch it, so she did. She wished she could get some words out, to thank him for meeting her, or ask where her mother was, but she couldn't. He was going to think she was pretty weird.

And she felt pretty weird. She felt as if she hadn't done anything wrong, except be black and grown up, which there

99

wasn't much she could do anything about; but she still felt ashamed, as if she'd done something wrong and was being punished.

The car pulled out of the parking lot and into traffic. The summer minister stopped talking and concentrated on driving through the city streets.

Mina looked straight ahead. "Your people mature earlier," that was what Miss Maddinton had said, but she didn't know what she was talking about. After Mina, the most physically mature girl in her class was white. Almost all the girls wore bras by the end of the sixth grade, not just black girls. Besides Kat didn't yet and she was black. Mina wished she'd said those things to Miss Maddinton. She wished she'd pushed Miss Maddinton out of the window, or something – done or said something to someone to let them know they couldn't push her around like this. Even though they could, because they did.

The car left the city on an elevated highway, moving along over the tops of row houses and stores. The highway merged with several other highways to form a new road, jammed with trucks and cars and heavy white heat. Stoplights came up, one after the other, quickly. At every one, brakes groaned and people honked their horns. All along the side of the road there were fast-food restaurants and motels and stores.

The summer minister, Alice's husband, drove on south. The signs overhead said Annapolis and Baltimore and Dover. He picked Dover, sticking to the main road. All the car windows were open, so it was cool enough when they were moving, although it was noisy from the motors working all around them.

Mina looked out her window, to catch the breeze and keep her face private. All of the feelings churning around inside her were looking for words so that she could understand them. But she couldn't find any words, and she didn't know why her mother hadn't come to meet her, because Momma could guess how she was feeling. She was heading home, but Mina didn't know what she'd be able to say when she got there.

She was sorry for all the things she'd thought. She was sorry for herself too, because they'd taken dance camp away from her. Because she wasn't good enough. Because she was black. She'd worked hard to be good enough, as hard as she could. But she couldn't work hard enough. She was disappointed in the people at camp and angry at them for not wanting her anymore. The same ideas ticked over and over inside her head, as the minutes ticked by and the car moved on south.

It was still a highway, but it had farms beside it now, except for crossroads where there would be a gas station, or a little restaurant. Mina wondered how far they'd gone, and how much time had passed. She felt the summer minister studying the back of her head. She felt him trying to start a conversation. But she didn't want to talk to him. If she didn't have any words for her family, she couldn't have anything at all to say to a perfect stranger. Mina concentrated on the fields they were passing, and the occasional house.

"So," she heard his voice begin. He had a quiet voice, deep. "How does it feel to be an ex-token black?"

Mina turned her head slowly to look at him. He had spoken words that connected so directly to her that she didn't know what to think. His eyes were on the road.

"A former token black? Or retired. Token black, retired," he said.

What a thing to say, Mina thought, as she burst out laughing and burst out crying, all at once together. Whenever the laughter was about to take over, Mina would remember how bad things were and the tears would continue. Whenever the tears started to dominate she would hear his voice asking her those questions and would keep up laughing.

"My wife usually has tissues in the glove compartment," he said after a while.

Mina needed several tissues before she finished with her nose and her eyes. She crumpled them up into her pocket when she was through.

101

"Thank you," she said. "I don't know what I'm going to do now," she told him.

He thought about that. "Do you mean now, here and now, or now, ever in your life?" He didn't wait for her to answer, which was just as well because Mina didn't know which she meant. She only knew it was true. "Your mother didn't come because she's sitting with Miz Hunter, who's had a bad summer virus. She's on the mend but when you're that old you've got to be careful with yourself."

Of course Momma would be there, helping out. Mina wondered why Alice didn't do it, to free Momma. But she couldn't ask him that, and she remembered that Alice had those three children, two of them pretty young.

"She's pretty. Your wife, I mean. I saw some pictures from last summer, and she's really pretty."

"Isn't she?" the man said, as if just thinking about Alice made him glad. "We've been married over nine years now, and every time I see her – I think, what fine work God did when he made Alice."

Mina liked the picture he made, of God up there like a sculptor, shaping the bodies and the faces.

"You know, you never answered me. Have you had lunch?"

"No," Mina said. "They gave me money for it, but I didn't."

"Are you hungry?"

"I think I am," Mina realised. It was mid-afternoon.

"If we pool our resources – I was up in Wilmington interviewing for a position and they gave me some travel expenses – I've got twenty dollars. How much do you have?"

"Five."

"How about it then, will you have lunch with me, Miss Wilhemina Smiths, whatever else you figure out you're going to do now?"

He really did understand, Mina thought. She thought she'd like to have lunch, and she liked this summer minister. He was funny.

"We can afford a respectable meal. They're not expecting us back until after supper anyway. There are some good restaurants around Easton. Can you wait for another forty-five minutes?"

"Sure. But I don't know your name. I wasn't listening when you said it. What is your name?" Mina asked. She was studying his profile now, as they drove along westward across Delaware. His hair was short, curling close to his head, and his eyes were set deep in their sockets. He had a broad mouth and good teeth, well-kept hands and long legs. He was a handsome man. His suit didn't look rumpled at all, even though the day was so hot and sticky.

"My name's Shipp. Tamer Shipp."

"Reverend Shipp," Mina repeated, trying the name on.

"I'd be more comfortable if you'd call me Tamer," he said

"I didn't mean—" Mina started to say.

"It's that name, 'reverend'. Because I have trouble feeling like – I should be reverend. You know?"

"It's not a name, it's a title," Mina pointed out, amused because he was taking words so exactly.

"A title's a kind of label. It's also a name, if you think about it."

Mina thought about it. She could see what he meant.

"Your father, now, I could call him 'reverend'. Though I've never met him, because he's always gone by the time I get here. I've met up with his work, over and over."

"What do you mean?"

"You can't step into a man's shoes, into this job like I do, into his life, and not learn a lot about him."

"I guess not," Mina said, thinking about the dancing slippers she had packed away in her suitcase. She planned to throw all that away as soon as she got home.

"I envy him, I think. My people—"

"Up in Harlem?"

"Harlem – the Harlem I see – the ghetto I serve – is down," he said." Down from everywhere. Wherever else you might be, if you go to Harlem you're going down."

He was being exact again. But he sounded tired when he said that, and his voice lost some of its richness. "I don't want to think about that right now," he said.

"Sure, Mr Shipp."

"The kids I know, the kids I work with, all call me Tamer."

"Even at home?"

"My home or your home?"

"Crisfield."

"Yep."

"Why?" Mina asked, before she thought to keep her mouth shut.

He didn't answer right away. Fields of corn, coming up green flowed past the car windows. The fields were edged by rows of trees, like high green fences. The sky, bleached white by summer heat, stretched out overhead. Mina figured, after a couple of minutes, that he wasn't going to answer her question.

But, "I can't think of why," he said, sounding surprised. "I've never thought about it, and I don't know why I didn't. Because I tend to think about things," he said.

"Oh," Mina said, not knowing what else to say.

"Drives Alice crazy." He turned to smile at her. There was something sure and strong about him, and his eyes, resting briefly on Mina, looked amused and interested and sympathetic. They looked knowing too, she thought, as if he knew a lot about her.

Mina was willing to bet that Momma had sent him up on purpose to meet her. But he said he'd had a job interview, so it couldn't have been that, and he said Momma was sitting with Miz Hunter, so she would have come with him if she could have. So it was just good luck he'd been the one, unless it was what her father called God's good time.

They had lunch in a little restaurant in the town of Easton, a couple of miles off Route 50. They were the only ones eating lunch at that hour. Mr Shipp thought Mina should order crab cakes, because she'd been away from crab country, but Mina explained about how when you were used to crab cakes as good as her mother's were, anything else wasn't worth the money. She had chicken instead. Mr Shipp couldn't decide. "My mother could give your wife the recipe," Mina said. "Or I could. They're easy."

He shook his head. "TV dinners are what Alice thinks of as easy. Roast chicken counts as hard. I'm hoping one of my girls will turn out to be a cook. I guess I'll compromise with stuffed shrimp." He smiled up at the waitress – who looked about thirty-five and worn out – who didn't smile back at him. "Baked potato, house dressing, and a glass of iced tea," Mr Shipp said, before she had to ask him. She nodded to show she'd heard, but her blue eyes never left the ticket she was writing. Mina watched her walk away, noting her thick-soled shoes and the bend of her neck, and the way she put her shoulder not her hand on the swinging door into the kitchen, as if she needed her shoulder's strength for the task of getting through that door. Mina got just a glimpse of the kitchen – long stainless counter and two black men at work.

"Did you notice her ring?" Mr Shipp asked her.

"She wasn't married."

"That faint mark, where her finger wasn't tanned. Like a ghost of a wedding band," he said. He took his water glass and drank it half down. "A woman her age, probably there are

105

children. I think an unreasonably large tip is in order, don't you?"

"Because you feel sorry for her?" Mina guessed.

"Because I know about how she feels," Mr Shipp corrected her.

"But Tamer," Mina said, his name uncomfortable in her mouth, "you're not divorced, are you?"

He shook his head.

"Have you been a waiter?"

He shook his head again, smiling, teasing, waiting for her to work it out.

"And you're not a woman, and you're not white."

He just waited.

"And I'm not going to call you Tamer, either; I'm going to call you Mr Shipp," Mina finished up.

He laughed then, and Mina joined in.

"You can't say I didn't try," he said. "So, are you beginning to look forward to getting home?"

Mina realised that she was. It was going to be all right, she realised.

They didn't hurry over their meal. They didn't dawdle. Mina had a slice of pecan pie for dessert, while Mr Shipp drank his coffee. They left almost ten dollars for a tip.

Back in the car, strapped in, back on the highway south, Mina asked him, "Did you get the job?"

"What job?"

"The one you interviewed for."

"Oh, that's right, I did have an interview. No, I don't think so."

"Did you want to get it?"

"Only partly. I keep thinking about my family living in Harlem, my kids growing up there, where there's little room to grow, and it's dangerous . . . Then I keep thinking about my work, and the people who destroy themselves because they think they're being destroyed. And they are too." It was anger she heard now. "I think about . . . what it is I'm meant to be doing. If that doesn't sound too conceited."

"No, it doesn't."

They travelled on without talking for some time. They went over the Choptank River, broad and blue at Cambridge. They crossed the little humped bridge at Vienna over the Nanticoke. The land flattened out around them and the air began to smell like home.

"Looks like there's been rain this summer," Mina said, breaking the long silence.

"There's been some good rainy days. I like this part of the world," Mr Shipp said, his head moving to watch a chicken farm go by his window. "I always did like it. I lived around here for a couple years when I was younger. For the last two years of high school," he answered her unspoken question, "when we first married, Alice and I."

"It's really different from Connecticut," Mina told him.

"Worse?"

"No, just really different. I like the hills and the trees up there, especially the trees. Connecticut is up, isn't it?"

"Definitely up," he answered. "You're finished with the grief then."

107

Mina wasn't surprised that he was understanding her. "I guess so. I guess it wasn't all that serious."

"Oh, I don't know." She watched his face. His skin fitted smooth over his forehead and cheekbones. He had a good strong jaw. "Some grief is sharp and sudden, and some is slower and longer. Sounds to me like you had the first kind, which is the easier – once it's behind you."

"Both would be pretty bad. Having both together."

He didn't answer, just nodded his head. Mina didn't know if this was to say he agreed with her, or just that he'd heard her. She wondered why he didn't answer, since he seemed to have something to say about almost everything. She wondered what he was remembering and understood that he didn't want to talk about it, so she changed the subject.

"I like this country too."

"Do you mean this country America? Or this country Dorchester County?"

"I mean Crisfield. I'm not too sure about America."

"Really? Because of being black? Because of slavery?"

"I don't know," Mina said, because she didn't. "I just don't feel comfortable, feel like I belong . . . I don't know." She'd never thought of that before, but it was true.

"I used to think, to wonder – I used to complain too, to Him – why God didn't lead us out of America the same way He'd led the Jews out of Egypt. There was a lot the same in the situations," Mr Shipp said.

"I guess there was," Mina said, thinking about it.

"I'd wonder why we didn't have any Moses. Then – if there was a Moses coming along. Dr King, I thought might be the man to lead us back to our own country."

"Except, of course, Moses wasn't black. The Jews weren't," Mina explained.

"Neither am I," Mr Shipp laughed.

Mina almost laughed. It had to be a joke. Then she saw it wasn't a joke.

She couldn't think of what to say. She wondered if he had a patch of craziness in him, that let him pretend to himself that he wasn't black. She thought she must have been wrong about him being strong and at peace, and that was depressing. She didn't know what she could possibly say to him now. Somehow, she knew that the one thing she felt like saying – "You are too!" – was the one thing she couldn't say. She turned her face to the fields again.

"But I'm not, Mina, and neither are you. Look at me. Look at yourself. We're not black, are we?"

Mina looked at the skin of her hands. It looked black to her. She looked back out of the window, embarrassed.

Between the rows of soybeans, the earth showed brown, the dark brown that meant rich soil, but lightened by the clay characteristic of this low land. This soil was dark, but not really black-brown like the soil where the bay ate away at the marsh grasses.

"I'm brown really," Mr Shipp said to her silence. "We are. Shades of brown. We call ourselves black because – the other words have been used and used derogatively. Negro – that's black too, in another language."

"Spanish," Mina mumbled, a little embarrassed at herself now.

"But I wouldn't like to be called 'brownie', would you?"

Mina giggled.

"Blacks, it's what we call ourselves, so that's all right."

"What would you rather be called?" Mina wondered.

"I always liked coloured," Mr Shipp said. "Because that covers just about everything."

Mina was looking at him again, and she saw he was half teasing. She thought about that, about all the colours the blacks were. There was dark, like Mr Shipp, dark, dark brown so that in certain lights you could see the purply black that went into it. Her skin was like a chocolate candy bar, a Hershey bar to be precise. Kat's had coppery tints in it. Some blacks were so light they were beige, almost, and some had golden tones and— She started to laugh, because he was exactly right about it.

"What's so funny?" he asked. But she was willing to bet he

already knew the answer.

"I'm not surprised you didn't get the job," she told him.

Mr Shipp's dark eyebrows went up, surprised, and his surprised laughter purred out of him into the warm air. "I'm going to have to watch out for you, Mina Smiths," he said. "You're—"

She waited.

He said what everybody had always been saying about her, all her life, except at camp. "You are t-roub-le."

Mina wished he'd said something else. Something different from what everybody else said.

Then he added. "I haven't known you but three hours, and already—"

"Already what?" she asked, when he didn't finish the sentence.

"Already you've got me talking with you like a friend," he said.

She was glad to hear him say that.

"I've got a congregation, and people I work with. I've got a family and a wife. But friends are in short supply. Unless maybe you count God, but I can't make out if He's my friend or what."

He didn't say that as if he minded not knowing, or even minded feeling as if he didn't have what he'd call friends. Mina didn't mind him thinking she was trouble, if that was how he thought about it.

She looked across at Mr Shipp, at his heavy, dark eyebrows and at his dark hands on the wheel of the car. There was a smile building up in her, of mischief and gladness and being free. They thought they were turning her out, turning their backs on her, but really they were sending her home.

THE GREATEST

MICHELLE MAGORIAN

"**B**OYS' GROUP," said the teacher.

The second group of girls broke away from the centre of the dance studio, their faces flushed, their skin streaming with sweat.

A skinny girl, whose fair hair was scraped up into a bun, smiled at him, and pretended to collapse with exhaustion against the *barre*.

"Kevin, aren't you a boy any more?" asked the teacher.

"Oh yes!" he exclaimed. "Sorry."

He joined the other three boys in the class. They were waiting for him opposite the mirror.

"You've been in a dream today," she said. "Now I expect some nice high jumps from you boys, so we'll take it slower. That doesn't mean flat feet. I want to see those feet stretched. First position. And one and two."

Kevin brought his arms up into first in front of him and out to the side to prepare for the jumps.

He loved the music the pianist chose for them. It made him feel as if he could leap as high and as powerfully as Mikhail Barishnikov. He knew that *barre* work was important but he

111

liked the exercises in the centre of the studio best, especially when they had to leap.

But today all the spring had gone out of him. A lead weight seemed to pull him down. Bending his knees in a deep *plié* he thrust himself as high as he could into the air.

"I want to see the effort in your legs, not your faces," remarked the teacher as he was in mid-spring.

They sprang in first position, their feet together, and out into second with their feet apart, then alternated from one to the other, out in, out in, sixteen times in each position, sixteen times for the change-overs.

"Don't collapse when you've finished," said the teacher. "Head up. Tummies in. And hold. Right everyone, back into the centre."

It was the end of class. The girls made wide sweeping curtsies, the boys stepped to each side with the music and bowed.

"Thank you," said the teacher.

They clapped to show their appreciation, as if they were in an adult class. Kevin knew that was what they did because in the holidays he was sometimes allowed to attend their Beginners' classes in ballet, even though he was only ten. He was more advanced than a beginner but at least the classes kept him fit.

Everyone ran to the corner of the studio to pick up their bags. It wasn't wise to leave any belongings in the changing-rooms. Too many things had been stolen from there.

The teacher stood by the door taking money from those who paid per class, or tickets from those whose parents paid for them ten at a time, which was cheaper.

Martin was standing in front of him, pouring out a handful of loose change into the teacher's tin. His father disapproved of boys or men doing ballet so Martin did it in secret and paid for his classes and fares by doing odd jobs. His only pair of dance tights were in ribbons and his dance shoes were so small that they hurt him.

Kevin handed his ticket to the teacher.

"I saw your father earlier on," she said. "Whose class is he taking?"

"He's not doing a class. It's an audition."

"Is that why your head is full of cotton wool today? Worried for him?"

"Not exactly," he said slowly.

He tugged at Martin's damp T-shirt.

"Dad gave me extra money today. I have to wait for him. Want some orange juice?"

"Yeah," said Martin eagerly.

"Let's grab a table."

They ran down the corridor to the canteen area and flung their bags on to chairs.

"I'm bushed," said Martin.

"Were you sweeping up Mr Grotowsky's shop this morning?"

"Yeah. And I cleaned cars. Dad thinks I'm working this afternoon, too."

"What if he checks up?"

"He won't. As long as he doesn't see me he doesn't care where I am."

"Doesn't he wonder why you don't have any money when you go home?"

"No. I tell him I spend it on Wimpy's or fruit machines."

Although he was only eleven Martin had already decided what he wanted to do with his life. He had it all mapped out. First he'd be a dancer, then a choreographer. His idol was a tall thin black American teacher in the Big Studio. He had performed in and choreographed shows in the West End. Professional dancers and students sweated and slaved for him, arching and stretching, moving in fast rhythms, leaping and spinning. There were black ones there too, like Martin. One day one of those black dancers would be him.

Some of the students were afraid of the teacher but they worked hard to be allowed to get into, and stay in, his classes.

"Get a classical training first," he had told Martin abruptly when Martin had plucked up enough courage to ask his advice. So that's what Martin was doing.

"What's the audition for?" he asked.

"A musical."

Kevin put their beakers of orange on the table.

"So what's the problem? Don't you think he has a chance?"

Kevin shrugged.

"Which one is it?"

"*Guys and Dolls*. He's going up for an acting part. He thinks his best chance of getting work as an actor is if he gets into a musical. He said no one will look at him if they know he's a dancer. He says directors think dancers haven't any brains."

"I'd like to see them try a class."

"Yes. That's what Dad says."

"Is it because you're nervous for him? Is that it?"

"No. We had a row this morning. We just ended up shouting at one another. We didn't talk to each other all the way here. Even in the changing-room."

"What was the row about?"

"About him auditioning for this job. I don't want him to get it."

"Why? He's been going to enough voice classes."

114

"Yes, I know," he mumbled.

For the last year his father had been doing voice exercises every morning, taking singing lessons, working on scenes from plays at the Actors' Centre, practising audition speeches and songs, and reading plays.

"I didn't think he'd have to go away, though. This theatre's a repertory theatre and it's miles away. I'd only see him at the weekend. And even then it'd probably only be Sundays. And if he got it he'd start rehearsing two weeks after I start school."

"So? You've been there before. Not like me. I start at the Comprehensive in a week's time. It'll be back to Saturday classes only." He swallowed the last dregs of his orange juice.

"Want another? Dad said it was OK."

"Yeah. I'll go and get them."

Kevin handed him the money and pulled on his track-suit top over his T-shirt even though he was still boiling from the class.

He couldn't imagine his father being an actor. But his father had explained that he couldn't be a dancer all his life, that choreographers would eventually turn him down for younger dancers and, in fact, had already done so a couple of times. He had to decide which direction he wanted to go in before that started to become a habit.

For the last two years, since Kevin's mother had died, his father had only accepted work in cabaret in London, or bit parts in films, or had given dance classes. Otherwise he had been on the dole. Kevin was used to him being around now.

When his mother was alive and his parents were touring with a dance company, Kevin used to stay with a friend of the family. Dad said it would be like old times staying with her again. Kevin didn't want it to be like old times. He wanted things to stay just as they were.

He pulled on his track-suit trousers, dumped his holdall on his chair and waved to Martin.

"I'll be back in a minute," he yelled.

He ran down the two flights of stairs which led to the

entrance hall, past two of the studios there and downstairs to the basement where the changing-rooms and other studios were.

Outside the studio where the audition was taking place stood a crowd of people peering in at the windows. They were blocking the corridor so that dancers going to and from the changing-room had to keep pushing their way through with an urgent, "Excuse me!"

The door to the studio opened and six disappointed men came out. Kevin's father wasn't among them.

Kevin squeezed in between two people by one of the windows and peered in.

Inside the steamed-up studio a group of men of every age, height and shape were listening to a woman director. A man was sitting at a piano.

The director was smiling and waving her arms about.

"Here. Squeeze in here," said a dancer in a red leotard. "You can see better. They're auditioning for *Guys and Dolls*. It's the men's turn today."

Kevin didn't let on that he knew.

"She's really putting them through it," said the dancer.

"First they have to sing on their own and the MD, that's the man at the piano, decides who's going to stay. Then they have to learn a song together."

"What's the song?" asked Kevin.

"*Luck Be a Lady Tonight*. Know it?"

Kevin nodded.

Know it? As soon as his father had heard he had been given the audition every song from *Guys and Dolls* had been played from breakfast to bedtime.

"Then they have to do an improvisation. The director chooses who to keep out of that lot and then the choreographer teaches them a dance routine."

The dancing would be kid's stuff for his father, thought Kevin. He wiped the glass. His father was standing listening. So, he'd passed two singing tests. Now it was the acting.

The director was obviously explaining what the scene was about. She was pointing to individual men.

"She's telling them about the characters," said the dancer.

Kevin felt angry. How could his father go through with it when he knew that Kevin didn't want him to go away? He observed his father's face, watched him grip his arms in front of himself and then quickly drop them and let out a breath.

"Excuse me!" he said fiercely, and he pushed himself out of the crowd and along the corridor to the stairs. And then he stopped. He remembered the look on his father's face and realized it was one of anxiety. It astounded him. He had seen his father upset before, but never scared. Why would he be scared? He was a brilliant dancer. But now, of course, he also needed to be a good actor. He was trying something new in front of actors who had been doing it for years and some of those actors were younger than him. That took guts, as Martin would say.

Kevin hadn't given a thought to how nervous his father might have been feeling. He knew how badly he missed the theatre. To start a new career when you were as old as him must be hard; harder too when he knew that Kevin hoped he would fail.

He turned and ran back down the corridor, ducked his head and pushed his way back into the crowd to where the dancer in the red leotard was standing. He wasn't too late. They hadn't started the improvisation yet. He stared through the glass willing his father to look at him.

The director stopped talking. The men began to move, their heads down in concentration as she backed away.

Please look this way, thought Kevin.

And then he did. He frowned and gazed sadly at him.

Kevin raised his thumb and mouthed, "Good luck!"

At that his father's face burst into a smile.

"Thanks," he mouthed back and he winked.

Kevin gave a wave and backed away through the crowd and along the corridor.

It was going to be all right, he thought. If his father did get the acting job he knew he'd be taken backstage and he'd meet lots of new people, and at least he wouldn't be touring so he could stay with him sometimes. And Martin could come too. And Dad would be happy again.

Martin wasn't at the table. Their bags were still there with the two plastic beakers of orange juice. Kevin knew where to find him. He walked to the corridor. Martin was gazing with admiration through one of the windows into the Big Studio. His idol was giving a class to the professional dancers.

He grinned when he saw Kevin.

"Guess what!" he squeaked. "I was by the door when he went in and he noticed me. And he spoke to me. He looked at my shoes and he said I ought to swap them for bigger ones at Lost Property and then, you know what he said? He said, "Say I sent you!""

He turned back to watching the class and sighed.

"Isn't he the greatest?"

"Yes," agreed Kevin, and he thought of his father. "Yes, he's the greatest."

WARTIME BALLET

MARGOT FONTEYN

from the autobiography of Margot Fonteyn

Margot Fonteyn, who died in 1991, was one of the most famous British ballerinas ever. Here she tells of her life as a young star of the Vic Wells Ballet (later the Sadler's Wells and now the Royal Ballet). The company, run by the formidable Ninette de Valois, also included the famous choreographer Frederick Ashton, the Australian dancer Robert Helpmann, and the renowned conductor Constant Lambert. It is 1939, and Margot has just met her future husband, Tito Arias.

I SAW LITTLE OF Tito in that last summer before the war. The die was now cast for my career, and even if he had suddenly, miraculously, declared his love and asked me to marry him, I believe I would have refused. I would have found it hard to relinquish my considerable foothold on the climb to success in my make-believe world in exchange for the realities of marriage and motherhood, the latter role presenting no attractions for me whatever. A chance remark by one of our Cambridge friends, intimating that Tito had been living with an American lady in Paris during the vacation, cut me deeply and confirmed the playboy tag with which I labelled him for the next fourteen years. I reckoned I had been mistaken in loving him. And that was that.

A short provincial tour before the new season had us all

119

hard at work dancing in every performance. I still took little notice of the war talk, even when a trial "blackout" of city lights was ordered for Saturday night as we closed our week in Liverpool. On Sunday morning the Sadler's Wells Ballet boarded a train to Leeds for our next engagement. As the train moved out of the station I thought I heard a porter shouting, "War declared!" as he ran along the platform closing the last doors. Tentatively, I mentioned this to the others in the carriage. "What, dear?" someone asked, so I repeated it. "Oh, rubbish. He was saying 'All clear', of course," said one of the adults. And so the matter was dismissed. It was 3 September 1939. Two and a half hours later we disembarked at Leeds, to learn that war had indeed been declared that morning. No one could believe it and most of us were too young to have much idea of what it meant anyway. Fred Ashton was silent and gloomy. Constant Lambert, untypically, was at a loss for an amusingly highbrow comment to fit the occasion, and even Helpmann could think of no way to turn this situation into absurdity.

War meant instant disaster and death; at least, that was how I imagined it as we stood about on the station platform wondering if the government would order all theatres to close immediately. Since the government had more urgent things to attend to first, we stayed overnight in a local hotel awaiting the decision. Pamela and I, sharing a room, were awakened in the night by the eerie sirens giving an air-raid warning. Of course I panicked, thinking that a bomb was on its way through the sky to me, personally, at that very minute. Unable to put the lights on for security reasons, we bumped about the bedroom, like bats in daylight, feeling for our clothes. In the dark I said to Pamela, "I can't find my things, let's wrap ourselves in the bedclothes and hurry down to the shelter." De Valois emerged from her room just as we were passing her door, swathed in blankets. "Don't be ridiculous, you two," she said. "Go back and get your dressing gowns at once." In the dusty cellar, which smelt of stale beer, a couple of hours passed while nothing at all happened to the city. Afterwards I felt extremely foolish about my hysterical behaviour.

We returned to London next day and the company was disbanded, since the government had after all decided to close places of entertainment. No one knew if and when theatres would be allowed to reopen. My mother was so calm I could not understand her. Why wasn't she making plans to leave London as quickly as possible? Why was she just sitting there waiting to see what would happen? In short, why wasn't she as frightened out of her wits as I was? She thought I should go off to the country to friends if I wanted to; she would stay in London as she had lived through World War I and didn't think there was such a desperate necessity to escape. Two weeks later the ballet was recalled to start immediately on a tour of undetermined length. Oh, what sore muscles and bruised toes we had as we went straight into performances without practising a step for fourteen days! The first week was physically painful, but soon our limbs accustomed themselves to dancing seven shows a week, which we continued to do for the next five years with only occasional short breaks. Engagements at military camps were not always well received by soldiers who did not think that war meant having to watch fancy ballet dancing. They banged their seats loudly to express their disgust as they left the theatre during the quietest moments of *Les Sylphides*, which was normally first in the programme. Some were heard to complain on the way out that it was more fun to spend the money on a postage stamp and write home. Others did not trouble to turn so delicate a phrase in expressing themselves. Most of this could be clearly heard on stage because the musical accompaniment came only from two pianos, one played by our conductor, Constant Lambert, and the other by our rehearsal pianist, Hilda Gaunt.

One night, in our theatrical lodgings, over cold meat, apple pie and hot tea, Fred Ashton announced that he was going to read the Bible from beginning to end, and that by the time he finished it the war would be over. Finding some passages monotonous and heavy going, he made a further announcement: he would read it aloud to us. Billie Chappell protested, saying: "Freddie, you can't do that to your friends." Nevertheless, Freddie did, but he miscalculated by about four years, and was to read a great many other books before the holocaust ceased.

During the "phoney war", so called because there were no attacks on England, it was arranged that in May 1940 the company should dance in Holland. There were some misgivings when we were about to depart, but an official came to tell us that we would be perfectly safe. Moreover, we should realize that our visit might be important in helping the morale of the Dutch people, who were so courageously facing our common enemy across their land frontier. So we set off cheerfully across the blessed English Channel, soon to save Britain from the fate of our allies on the mainland.

In The Hague an extraordinary calm masked the tensions of a country that sensed its imminent fate and wondered only when and where the first blow would fall. Perhaps the arrival of an English ballet company, laughing and sightseeing for all the world as though nothing unusual was going on, did indeed ease the spirits of some people, for our opening performance was received with almost heartbreaking enthusiasm, and tulips were rained upon us from above as we took the last curtain calls. There was an exceptional bond of intimacy between performers and public that night, as both sides joined in an elaborate pretence, never admitted, that time could be made to stand still and impending doom held for ever at bay.

The gravity of the situation became more obvious every day. The generation above mine reacted according to their different temperaments. De Valois showed her anxiety only when caught off guard. Constant Lambert tried to look cheerfully fatalistic. Ashton's hypersensitive imagination worked like an antenna to pick up new signs of the impending German invasion. Helpmann, the court jester, wrapped truth in humour in order to break the tension he perhaps felt more than anyone else. He made a joke out of

everything so that even de Valois, who felt personally responsible for the whole troupe, relaxed and laughed, particularly when he said that the covered barges we saw on the canals were packed with German soldiers dressed as nuns with machine-guns concealed under their habits – which, for all I know, may have turned out true though we all thought it just a hilarious fantasy.

On the fourth day we danced at Arnhem, getting there early enough to see something of the town before going into the theatre. In the afternoon sun we stood on the bridge looking towards Germany. "The frontier is only half an hour in that direction," said our guide. "Half an hour by car or ten minutes by tank!" said Helpmann. "Now I understand why they decided to send us straight back to The Hague tonight instead of tomorrow morning." The journey back was very slow, due to the sudden flood of armoured vehicles coming towards us in the small hours of the morning. "It must be a general mobilization. They are all going to the border." In our darkened bus we all fell silent. Even Helpmann was serious.

At dawn there was a sudden commotion in the hotel corridors. "Invasion. The Germans are invading; they are landing by parachute all around us." Someone found that the roof offered a perfect lookout, and indeed it was a fascinating and rather beautiful sight as the earliest rays of sun caught the distant parachutes like little puffs of silver smoke, slowly sinking down and vanishing beyond the city skyline. A brisk burst of gunfire sent us scampering down the stairs, and we were soon ordered to the cellars. But, as the day wore on, groups ventured out to the square to sit in the sun. Again, exposure was short-lived. A single bullet, narrowly missing Fred and Bobby in a sidewalk café, provoked an order that everyone must stay inside the hotel until instructions were received from the British Embassy. Only de Valois and Lambert went out to discuss with the Ambassador and the Dutch authorities what could be done. A suggestion that the girls could return to England, leaving the men behind, was brusquely dismissed by de Valois. Hours passed. All was tranquil on the surface. Rumours, alerts, counter-rumours, cancellations: "Arnhem fell early this morning"; "Be ready to leave in half an hour"; "We can't leave, the transport has been commandeered"; "More divisions have landed."

The following night two buses drew up in front of the hotel. We clambered aboard, taking with us only what we could wear and with no clue to the destination of our journey. At the front and rear of each bus was a young soldier, well armed. One of them tried to converse in short phrases, using German words among the Dutch. We had difficulty in getting the gist of what he said: "*Juda; nicht aryan.*" Then we realized he was telling us that he was Jewish. He must have felt such a need to communicate with friendly people in that unlit bus, which halted every few yards on its way through the ink-black night. "Poor boy!" we thought. "He is certain of death at German hands." We were suddenly aware how cold it was in the bus.

Perhaps the ride lasted six hours; anyway, it was still dark when we halted for the last time. Everyone was happy to unfold stiff limbs and enter a large château, but since it was overcrowded with other refugees we went out to walk a little before trying to find a corner in which to lie down. The faintest grey light was breaking through the dense night sky. We were in a big garden. The chilly air was sweet and fresh, and trees took shape as the light grew. Slowly there came the miraculous unfolding of a picture so serene and exquisite, touched with morning dew and the promise of a fine warm day. It was like a Japanese landscape. A mist-laden lake, rushes, flowering shrubs, pathways and broad lawns came into view as the first vigilant birds alerted others to the hour of awakening. These stirrings of dawn quickly provoked more movement by the water's edge, as a variety of ducks shook ·their feathers, while herons, treading with extreme care, delicately lowered their long legs and stirred life into some deer who softly stretched and wandered away into the park to start a day that, for them, would not be different from any other.

The day we spent in this blissfully rural paradise was disturbed by occasional bursts of gunfire and rumours that, by a new landing of the enemy, the area was encircled. There was nothing anyone could do, so some of the company organized a game of football with the Dutch soldiers, for all the world as though it were midsummer's day on the village green.

With nightfall our buses moved on again, haltingly as before, until we reached a quayside where we joined a long queue of people waiting to board the ship that was tied up alongside. We were at the port of Ijmuiden, though there was no way of finding that out at the time. Docks and harbours were obvious targets for enemy bombers, and it was an unpleasant feeling edging along in a queue, wondering why those in front couldn't hurry themselves so that we at the back could get under cover, too. Once on board we sailed immediately; I didn't know that a ship could get away so speedily.

The English Channel was mined, and one's instinct was to stay up on deck with the chance of landing on the surface and floating if trouble came. Of course, there was no space, and everyone was ordered below decks. It transpired that we were not in a passenger ship at all. The huge gloomy area of the aft

hold was already crowded with women and children, settled on the floor; one could hardly look around for a small space and get down likewise on the hard boards among the straw, imagining the horror that would follow if we were blown up. Such thoughts, together with the cold and discomfort, didn't encourage sleep. But at last the night gave way to another fair day, and we sailed into the safety of Harwich and home.

Back home at long last I recounted it all to my mother, then fell fast asleep for twenty-four hours.

The "phoney war" was over. Holland was overrun and defeated in five days; we had been among the last to get out. The horror in Europe spread from East to West; the disaster of Dunkirk seemed almost a victory, and Britain took up her solitary stand behind the English Channel.

Often during those days I tried to remind myself how lucky I was. I was distressed to find how much I cared about material things such as my books and little ballet treasures, including my photographs of the old ballerinas. I really did not want to lose these things, and yet I was ashamed to hold such petty thoughts when there was agonizing human suffering all about me.

For what was I doing all this time? Dancing! I remained in my chosen profession, with little privation or real discomfort, and without losing any close relation. Even my friends were spared, with the exception of Painton Cowan, who had fallen in love with Pamela May in those happy Cambridge days. When the war came they married, like thousands of other couples, to try to snatch at least a few moments of happiness. Painton was killed three weeks after their son was born.

In the ballet we became an even more closely knit family. Most of the men were called up to do national service, Michael Somes among them. His case was typical: he was away for four years, from the age of 23 to 27, perhaps the most vital period for a dancer. But after it was all over he struggled back into training, shrugging off philosophically the disruption of his career like all of them. Ninette de Valois was adamant in her refusal to invite as guest artists any of the new young dancers from abroad who, not having lost a slice of their careers, were then more inspiring to watch. Said de Valois emphatically, "I will not do it. If I take any of these foreign boys it will discourage our own dancers and we will never develop a tradition for male dancers in England. It is not fair to our boys."

Frederick Ashton, being a true creative artist, had quickly absorbed the impact of war. Even before our visit to Holland, he produced *Dante Sonata*, which he saw as a struggle to the death between The Children of Light and The Children of Darkness. It was created in the modern dance idiom in bare feet, and we were for ever coaxing splinters out of our bodies, since there was a lot of dragging each other across the stage and no one ever thought to lay a covering over the ancient wooden floorboards of English provincial theatres. But we felt so deeply the passion for Ashton's heart-cry for humanity that we cared nothing for the splinters. It was a ballet impossible to reproduce after the war, danced by a generation too young to understand the time of its creation.

Dante Sonata was conceived during the "phoney war". The next phase, that of bombing the cities, brought a different Muse to Ashton's side, and he choreographed an exquisite ballet called *The Wise Virgins*, based on the biblical parable. It was an escape to spiritual thoughts in a time of human agony. This ballet, too, we performed with intense fervour – though there was a lot of mirth when we saw it advertised on a billboard as "*The Wise Virgins* (subject to alteration)".

As more and more male dancers were called up, so boys were taken early from the school to give them, and us, two years of their dancing before they reached eighteen and went to fight. Naturally, they were not the strongest partners, and the girls learned to fend for themselves in those pirouettes called "supported" in which their partners should help them. Lifts were another matter, and I was not alone in being nervous when thrown into the air by these youngsters!

The person who more than any other kept the company

going during the war was Robert Helpmann. Not only did he support our morale with his humour, he was the one star who could help the company reach dancing maturity. While Fred Ashton was serving as an officer in the Air Force, Helpmann began to create ballets, of which *Hamlet* is definitely a masterpiece, while the others were all original and exciting theatrical experiences. It was a godsend to us that, as an Australian, he was not called up.

De Valois, meanwhile, remained a supreme leader. We would one and all unhesitatingly defend her and obey her commands. We would, metaphorically speaking, have died for her. Part of her secret, like that of all great generals, was that she cared deeply about our lives and our personal problems as well as our careers, although it took me a long time to find that out. It was Gordon Hamilton who decreed that she should and must be addressed as Madame, not Miss de Valois. So she has been Madame to her dancers ever since and in that form still signs her letters to me, but in quotes, thus, "Madame".

Like most people in wartime, we had little in the way of personal lives. We spent long hours in the theatre, and we alternated provincial tours of eight to ten weeks with shorter seasons in London. I still did not feel very grown-up, though I had passed my twenty-first birthday, but at least I was no longer afraid of the others. Helpmann, Ashton and Chappell were Bobby, Freddie and Billie; their dressing rooms were always ringing with laughter. One evening Bobby ran into my room to tell me the latest, somewhat indecent, cause of amusement, and then stopped suddenly: "I wonder," he said, as he looked at me in the mirror putting on my make-up, "if Karsavina and Nijinsky used to tell funny stories in the dressing room, too?" Somehow the idea seemed sacrilegious.

Outside the theatre, life became more and more drab, food less and less adequate. This was a problem because of the energy that dancers burn up. Ballet fans were marvellous about sending little parcels of sugar, chocolate, butter and other rationed food, depriving themselves of their own very meagre allowance to help us. I missed the butter more than anything, for the two ounces allowed per week was the amount I had previously eaten at one breakfast. We started looking for other sources of energy and drank lashings of a strange green tonic which was described as "giving you tomorrow's strength today". All that happened was that tomorrow we felt even more tired, and drank more green drink. Dancing every night with three matinées made a very heavy week, so as an experiment the Thursday afternoon show was moved over to Saturday, giving us three performances that day. But at least we had all Sunday to recover. The three Saturday performances had to run nonstop, with only a half-hour between them, in order to finish early enough for the public to reach home before the bombs fell. After one or two girls had fainted on stage, this Saturday schedule was abandoned. I was quite sorry. It had been rather fun, in a way, while it lasted.

Pamela May was away from the ballet for quite a while having her baby. June Brae, the other member of our "triptych", had met David Breeden at Cambridge at the same time that I met Tito and Pamela met Painton. June and David married early in the war, and their daughter was born soon after Pamela's son. I seemed to be the odd girl out.

Alone in No. 1 dressing room, without my closest friends, I developed a star complex, and for a time I was really impossible, imagining that I was different from, and superior to, those around me. Then Pamela came to see us. It was soon after she had been widowed. Completely broken up by her loss, and living as she did facing up to stark reality, she was in no mood to put up with my fanciful airs. She told me outright that I had become a bore. Thinking it over, I decided that I far preferred the company of my friends to the isolated pinnacle implied by the title Prima Ballerina Assoluta, which I had been trying to reach, so I climbed down. As a matter of fact, it had been partly the fault of what I call false friends – those who, with the best will, and believing themselves your warmest admirers, unwittingly destroy you with such talk as: "People don't realize how great you are"; "You are the greatest ballerina alive; people should fall back in awe when you leave the stage door"; "You should be treated like a queen." All of which is, of course, rubbish. Great artists are people who find the way to be themselves in their art. Any sort of pretension induces mediocrity in art and life alike.

I received some sad stage-door calls. A few months after the Dunkirk debacle. I was told by the stage doorman that two ladies were asking to see me. "They say they are good friends of your husband; he stayed with them after Dunkirk." "But I haven't got a husband," I said. He looked concerned. "I think you should see them; they are sure you will know them." So they came in and I learned how a soldier had been billeted with them for several months and how he had said I was his wife. They were very fond of him and showed me his picture taken in the garden with the family and the dog. It was hard for them to believe the truth. Indeed, I hated to upset them, and I have often thought sadly of the boy, so obviously lonely and lost. This sort of episode was not uncommon.

A little old lady came to my dressing room in London. At first I thought she wanted a job as wardrobe mistress, but her conversation ruled that out. "This is something that will help you very much; many people have been helped." She didn't say what it was, but I guessed it must be religion. "Well, thank you very much, but I think I am all right," I said. She persisted, however, and suddenly asked, "You know Miss So-and-so, the Chinese dancer, don't you?" "No I'm afraid I don't," I replied, thinking, *Well, it can't be religion so whatever is it?* "Yes, I know you know her. She has been helped very much by this, too." Eventually I got rid of the lady, still mystified by her visit until I realized the only possible explanation was that she peddled drugs and had mistaken me for someone else. It was an alarming occurrence.

"There's a G.I. asking to see you," said the doorman one day. That was a surprise, too, for although London was full of G.I.s, I had not met one. "Shall I show him in?" I was intrigued, so I said, "Yes." He introduced himself as Joseph Stuhl from Philadelphia. "I saw you dancing tonight," he said. "It was marvellous. I've brought a box of chocolates for you. I know they are rationed here." He was a charming young man, so well-mannered and correct. It happened that he came to the ballet on D-Day, and crossed to Europe the next morning, so I did not realize at the time that I had made a lifelong friend. He was the first of many American friends, whom I have found the kindest in the world.

The only other encounter I had with an American soldier was once as I was going home in the blackout after the ballet. I did not like the drunken crowd around Piccadilly tube station, so I decided, even though I was fairly frightened of the unlit street, to walk to Green Park station. I always walked close to the curb, not liking the idea that someone might jump out from a dark doorway and grab me. I heard footsteps close behind, so I moved a little faster. The footsteps came nearer and I hurried even more. Just as I turned to enter the station, a gentle American voice said, "Pardon me for speaking to you. I just wanted to say that I noticed you are the only girl in

Piccadilly tonight who isn't trying to get picked up." "Oh, thank you," I said. "Good-night." And he replied "Good-night," very politely. I thought he was an officer, but I never saw his face because there was no moon that night.

In the days – or rather, nights – of the blitz we welcomed moonless nights. But then came a new horror, which cared for neither moon nor sun. The buzz bombs. They came through the sunny skies, their engines making plenty of noise so that everyone would know death was approaching. As in a game of musical chairs, one listened for the moment when the music stopped and, if it seemed overhead at the time, one dived behind the settee and hoped for the best. One might not be able to do much about a direct hit, but it would be silly to be caught by the flying glass if it only landed nearby. After the buzz bombs came the V2s, which landed indiscriminately without any warning. But throughout the war, no matter what happened I never heard of anyone getting up from his or her seat to leave the theatre because of an air-raid alert.

I was reminded of this period, and of our spirit, when I came across a letter I had written on 28 June 1944.

Dearest Grandma and Auntie,

I expect you will be worrying about us in the raids which are none too pleasant I must say. However, we are absolutely safe and well so far despite the fact that the house has been blasted to bits, more or less, on Monday night at 12 o'clock. I was out and missed all the fun but Mother was by the front door which gave her a slight bang on the backside before landing up against the wall. The bomb hit the top of a big block just opposite us in the main road, about 200 yards away, and the blast has broken every window but one in the house and removed most of the doors, part of the roof and brought down part of the ceilings and walls, so it is in a pretty state. Rather draughty in this weather! And the dirt and mess are unbelievable. But practically nothing is broken, no furniture, glass or china. I just can't understand it. Poor Mother is in the throes of trying to clean up the mess. She is really wonderful about it, having had no sleep Monday night and worked ever since. She is rather tired and getting a slight reaction today but is cheerful. It all might have been much worse and where we are at the moment is as safe as anywhere else. Certainly downstairs is the place to be as the blast goes upwards and the bombs almost always explode on impact with the top of a building so don't worry about us.

The theatre is still full every night.

Must go to bed now.

All my love,
Margot.

At the outbreak of war my mother had initially leased an Elizabethan house in the country to avoid the expected air raids. When they became routine she moved back to London, knowing that she could not miss all those performances and that I needed home cooking and comforts. Every bit of my energy went into dancing, and she did the rest.

Felix was in the Army, where in the course of time his mechanical skill and patience, inherited from our father and grandfather, were put to work on testing new tank weapons. For his peacetime photographic career he had adopted the name of Fonteyn, at my suggestion.

My father had been able to see some of my early Sadler's Wells performances when he came home on leave in 1936. His next leave, due in 1940, was postponed indefinitely because of the war, so that we did not see him at all for ten years. When the Japanese overran Shanghai he was among the enemy aliens taken into internment camp, where on his arrival he wisely volunteered for kitchen duties and spent the next two and a half years boiling rice but remaining cheerful and adequately fed.

Among the marvellous "fans" who sent bunches of flowers, and still do to this day, were two sisters, Charlotte and Irene Armspach. I had not met them but knew their names well from their many little messages of goodwill. So, when a young sailor wrote asking if I could occasionally send him some news of the ballet, which he greatly missed now that he was in the Mediterranean, I forwarded his letter to them suggesting that they might write. My scheme had the happiest result. Sidney Dawlson, the sailor, and Charlotte later married, and I still hear from them whenever I dance in London. I was also flattered to hear that my photograph hung in the Officers' Ward Room of H.M.S. *Aurora*, because of my role in *The Sleeping Beauty*.

In ordinary life, elegance had all but disappeared with the shortages and rationing of fabrics. Our silk stockings were sent for repair again and again to the countless little shops where girls sat in the windows invisibly mending the runs. In the ballet we were quite adept at picking up the ladders in our irreplaceable silk tights, using little hooks. It was a slow job, but it restored them perfectly. Before the Dunkirk retreat some friends in the Navy had been able to buy a supply of tights from the maker in Paris and had smuggled them into England, and these were made to last out the duration of the war. Most fortuitous of all, the ballet-shoe makers were permitted the necessary materials to continue their trade.

There were rumours of a remarkable new fibre called nylon, which could be made into stockings that would never wear out. This was not true, of course, but the real difference was that nylon is very much finer than the sheerest silk imaginable. Until that time, all ballet shoes were made in pure silk slipper satin, which has a sheen finish unmatched by any artificial material. I have always steadfastly insisted on pure silk for my shoes, with double satin ribbons to tie round the ankle. I also insist on silk ballet tights. The ribbon is virtually unobtainable these days, and now the manufacture of silk tights has been discontinued. Since, after so many years, I cannot accustom myself to dance in any others, this might just turn out to be the factor that will finally decide my retirement.

THE SWAN MOTHER

JEAN RICHARDSON

BIRTH MOTHER, I think that's what they're called nowadays, to distinguish them from the kind of mothers who bring you up and do all the things mothers are supposed to do, like being there when you need them and knowing what you really want for your birthday. I'd never thought much about my birth mother, which I suppose shows how successful my stepmother was at making me feel she was my real mum – until I started dancing.

Actually it was her idea that I should go to dancing classes. I suspect she thought it was something nice for a little girl to do, and easier than riding, which could end up with my demanding a pony. But what she didn't foresee or understand was the effect that dancing had on me. I was mad about it. I practised for hours every day, far more than was good for me, and I used to put my pink satin ballet shoes on the window-sill so that they were the first thing I saw every morning. Mum accused me of wanting to live in a leotard, and my brothers – well, stepbrothers really – called me "Little Swan" and fell about laughing whenever there was any ballet on television.

But I didn't mind. Dancing gave my life a shape as satisfying as an *arabesque* – that beautiful position where you have one leg raised behind you and hold your arms so as to make a continuous line from your fingertips through to your toes. If other people can't understand how wonderful it is to find something you can do really well, too bad. They're only jealous.

For I am good. I got top grades in my exams and couldn't help knowing, however conceited it sounds, that I was the best pupil at the Romanoff ballet school (which had nothing Russian about it apart from its name). The principal, Mrs Burnett, who'd once been in the *corps de ballet* and loved telling us about Anthony and Antoinette, thought I was good enough to get a place at one of those special schools where you get full time training.

I thought Mum and Dad would be pleased – parents are supposed to want you to take things seriously – but Dad hated the idea. I probably get my strong will from him, and I was determined to get my way. There were rows and sulks and once, when I lost my temper and screamed at him, he said with frightening fury that I was just like my mother. And that was what first made me think about my birth mother.

I don't remember her at all because I was only a few months old when she went away. There are no photographs of her, and my father never talks about her. It's as though he's always been married to my stepmother and any earlier marriage was just a bad dream.

Once I began to think about her, I had this strange feeling that she would have understood why dancing mattered so much to me. I wondered if, perhaps, she could have been a dancer. It might explain why Dad seems so hostile to dancing, and why he always sides with the boys when they make fun of it. I've sometimes seen a look on his face that I couldn't understand, but maybe dancing, and dancers, bring back painful memories.

I got my own way about the school, but although it isn't a boarding-school, being there has cut me off from the family.

They aren't interested in what happens in class, what it feels like when I do a movement really well, or how devastating it seems when I can't memorise a difficult sequence. They don't realise how it stings to be criticised, or how frightened I am of growing too tall like Karen or the wrong shape like Angela. They've both been asked to leave at the end of term. When I hurt my ankle, Mum made as much fuss of me as she did of Tom when he injured himself playing silly football, but she couldn't see that my injury was more than a painful knock, that it could have meant the end of my career.

But my birth mother understood. Her startling blue eyes, a grown-up version of mine, were full of concern, because she knew from her own experience how terrified dancers are of being injured.

I can't explain how I seemed to know what she looked like, but I recognised her at once when I saw her photograph in a newspaper.

It was under the headline A SWAN FLIES BACK – I think it was the word "swan" that caught my eye – and it showed the dancer Francesca Shaw arriving at Heathrow airport. According to the story, she had once been the great hope of British ballet, a potential Margot Fonteyn, but then she'd gone to America and never come back. Until now. Friends and colleagues were said to be delighted that she was at last returning to dance in *Swan Lake*, and faithful fans were already queuing for tickets.

I knew at once that I had to see her dance. But how? I thought of asking if I could go as an advance birthday present, but I'd only just had a birthday. Perhaps the school would get tickets, we were sometimes invited to special events, but it might not be my turn. I was sitting on the stairs, trying to work out how I could possibly get a ticket, when I heard my name and realized my parents were talking about me. I didn't mean to listen, but when I took in what they were saying, I didn't seem able to move.

"But Jenny has a right to see her, she really does." That was my stepmother. "After all, she is her mother."

They were talking about HER.

"In theory, yes." That was my father. "But what sort of a mother has she been! She's never taken any interest in Jenny and now, just because she's over here for a few weeks, she wants to meet her."

"It's only natural. I'm sure I'd feel the same if it was one of the boys."

"But you didn't abandon a child for another man when it was only a few weeks old." My father sounded so bitter. "By my reckoning, she forfeited all rights to Jenny, and turning up now will only upset her."

"Maybe, but we must help her cope with it. You don't have the right to stop them meeting. If you do, Jenny may blame you one day. Children always want to find out about their real parents, however good the substitute ones are, and Jenny's at an age to start thinking about things like that."

"She's never mentioned her mother. Or asked about her."

"But that doesn't mean she hasn't thought about her."

I don't know what Dad said next, because I went back upstairs to my room. I didn't feel comfortable eavesdropping, and in a strange way I felt guilty because I already knew far more than they guessed. It was as though I'd grown up when they weren't looking. Certainly there was no way now that I could ask them to take me to see Francesca Shaw dance. That was something I had to do by myself.

I haven't been to the ballet that often, mainly because when we do go to a theatre, it's for a family treat, and neither Dad nor the boys want to see a ballet. But I've read so much about ballets that I feel as though I've seen them, and this year I'll probably get a chance to appear in *The Nutcracker*, as the school has an arrangement with a company that stages it every Christmas.

I phoned the theatre where Francesca was dancing and asked about tickets. The man in the box office said I should write in stating dates and prices and enclosing a cheque or my credit card number. I panicked, said I couldn't possibly do that, and he then became much more human and said I could buy a ticket from the box office, providing I came along on the day that booking opened. Of course it had to be a Wednesday, which meant missing class – that's the day we concentrate on *pointe* work – and going to the West End by myself, which I'm not supposed to do. What fusspots parents are!

The queue seemed endless: the length of the theatre and round into the next street. The nice thing, however, was that everyone was so friendly. They chatted about how early they'd had to get up and how far they'd come, who they'd seen in *Swan Lake* and how wonderful Francesca Shaw was.

"She was the finest Odette I've seen – and I've seen Makarova," boasted an elderly man. "You don't see that kind of star quality often. It was a tragedy when she left us."

"Something to do with a boyfriend, wasn't it?" This was a woman in a woolly hat. "I heard she was very unhappy."

"Perhaps you have to be unhappy to dance that well," suggested the elderly man gently. "There was real feeling in her dancing, which is more than you can say for most of them nowadays. It's all technique."

I wanted to say, I nearly said, "Francesca Shaw's my mother," but they would have wondered why I was queuing for a ticket and looked at me curiously. So instead I asked if they thought we'd be lucky.

"Should be, but at a price." And that set them off reminiscing about how cheap the seats used to be, and how disgraceful it was to pay so much now even to sit in the gods.

By the time we reached the box office, there weren't any balcony seats. "Do you a side stalls for £30, or a little further in if you don't mind a matinée," said a boy with bleached locks and cheeky eyes.

"You are sure Francesca Shaw will be dancing at a matinée?"

"Money back if she isn't," said the boy, offering to cross his heart as well.

The ticket swallowed up nearly all my savings, and it was goodbye to those black boots that I so wanted and Mum didn't approve of, but they could wait. I was willing to

sacrifice anything to see my mother dance.

Going to a matinée was much easier than an evening performance would have been, though it did mean more time off school with another migraine. I do have them quite often, especially if I get over-excited, so I did wonder if I might be punished for all this deceit with a real brain-storming head-ache.

The school secretary was embarrassingly sympathetic. "You should try those new pills. I'm told they really do work if you take them in time."

"I'm OK, honestly. I'll be all right if I go home now, before the flashing lights start."

That really upset her, and I was afraid she'd insist on coming with me, but luckily the phone rang and I was able to slip away.

I got to the theatre far too early, and all the things I normally enjoy, reading my programme, looking to see who's in the boxes, pretending the audience is waiting to see me, only irritated me. I sat there willing the curtain to go up.

It was my first *Swan Lake*, but I knew the story and watched impatiently as Prince Siegfried was given a crossbow and decided to hunt swans with his friends. When the swans appeared, Siegfried followed them on his own and was surprised to see one of them turn into a beautiful girl.

Francesca was so slight and fragile, like swansdown. I absolutely believed that she was a princess who'd been bewitched by a wicked enchanter. I'd tried dancing to that haunted, passionate music ever since I first heard it, but never like this.

The intervals were agony. I didn't want a drink or an ice, and I couldn't bear the way everyone round me was chattering. They seemed so unmoved by what had happened on stage.

In the next act, it was as though I was dancing with Francesca, step by step, sharing her speed and precision, the ease with which the famous thirty-two *fouettés* sprang from her feet as the climax to the glittering wickedness of the false

Odile. She unfolded the music, following its line so closely that the notes seemed to flow from her feet. I don't know how a critic would describe this: for me, it was simply magic. At the end – and I stayed for all the curtain calls, clapping and stamping to make Francesca come back just one more time – I knew beyond all shadow of doubt that I had to be a dancer.

I drifted home in a dream of rustling white gauze, as skeins of swans crisscrossed the stage and parted to admit – was it Francesca, or me?

I was late for tea, but I wouldn't eat anything and I didn't want to talk.

"Sure you're all right?" Mum asked. "It's not like you to turn down a jacket potato."

"I'm not hungry, that's all. I think I'll go upstairs." I didn't want any more questions.

I lay on my bed thinking about Francesca, and then got up to look in the mirror with my programme open at the picture of her. Were we alike? There was a knock at the door, and Dad asked if he could have a word. He's good about not barging in. I stuffed the programme in my dressing-table drawer and lay down again.

"You all right?" I do love him when he looks concerned.

"Sure. I thought I might be getting a headache, that's all."

He sat on the bed and seemed lost for words. "Sweetheart, I want to talk to you about something I ought to have mentioned ages ago."

I couldn't imagine what he was going to say. We'd done the facts of life – well, Mum had – years ago.

"It's my fault," he said, looking down. "but we've been such a happy family that I didn't want to spoil things by bringing up the past. And you've never asked about your mother."

He must have found out about this afternoon.

"Look, Jen, when your mother went to live in America, I didn't think she'd ever come back. I thought . . . Mum and I thought, a complete break would be better for you. Now, out of the blue, she's over here on a flying visit and has asked to see you. I've told her that it must be your decision. It's up to you. Do you want to see her?"

Did I want to see Francesca Shaw! How little Dad knew me if he needed to ask that. I wondered what he'd say if I told him that we'd already met, that we'd danced *Swan Lake* together?

"Yes, yes I do." The words didn't sound very gracious, but I've never been very good with words. Perhaps that's why I feel so alive when I'm dancing.

"Your mother's here on business and seems to have a very busy schedule. She's suggested this Saturday afternoon, but I gather you're dancing in some show."

Some show! It was a gala in aid of a new studio for the Romanoff school, and Mrs B. had asked me as the school's star ex-pupil: the one who'd made it to a real ballet school. I couldn't possibly let her down.

I'm not sure Dad understood this. I suspect he thought I was upset at the thought of meeting my mother.

"It doesn't have to be a problem," he said, and his voice was so gentle that I flung my arms round him and hugged him like I used to when I was little. "As dancing takes up so much of your life," he went on, stroking my hair, which he never does now I'm grown up, "I thought it would be nice for her to see you dance. Then you can meet each other afterwards, and you'll have something to talk about." I must have tensed, because he added, "I mean . . . of course you'll have lots to talk about, but dancing might help to get you started."

Dear, silly, Dad!

I was much too excited to sleep, and I lay awake thinking how everything would change. I pictured myself at school, mentioning quite casually, that I'd seen Francesca Shaw in *Swan Lake* and that she wanted to see me dance because she was – wait for it – my real mother! I'd sometimes envied girls who had "ballet mothers" – the kind who sew costumes and sit around for hours minding your gear and rubbishing everyone else, something Mum is much too nice to do – but I'd never known anyone whose mother was a ballerina. I wondered too what she would feel watching her daughter dance.

My solo had been planned as the climax of the gala, which began with the tinies pretending to be circus ponies galloping round the ring. I'm still fond of the Romanoff school, but it did suddenly seem very amateur and I hoped Francesca wouldn't be too bored. I was tempted to look for her in the audience, but I felt it might make me even more nervous, so I kept out of sight backstage.

Mrs B. had arranged a Chopin waltz and mazurka from *Les Sylphides* for my solo, and I was wearing the classic long white dress with a circle of rosebuds in my hair. Some of the younger girls looked at me with that mixture of jealousy and admiration I remember feeling at their age, and when the curtains parted there was a murmur of approval from the audience.

When I started to dance, I felt as though I had split into two: part of me was in charge of my feet, the way I held my arms, the way I carried my head, while the other part responded to the music and the poetry of the steps. I knew that I had never danced better, and if most of the audience just thought I was a pretty little girl, one person at least would really appreciate me.

There was applause, and the tiniest tot presented me with a bouquet, but it seemed like a dream leading up to the moment when I'd at last come face to face with Francesca Shaw. I wanted to get changed, but it wasn't easy in the scrum backstage, where I kept being stopped by well-meaning aunties and grannies determined to say a few words of praise.

I was nearly ready by the time Dad managed to find my corner. With him was a smartly dressed woman whose face was partly hidden by tinted glasses. She looked at me hesitantly and then said with a slight American accent, "Honey, you were terrific. I don't know where you get it from, because I can't dance a step, but you were the star of the show and I'm very proud of you."

I couldn't take in what she was saying. Who was she, this total stranger? I heard my father say, "Your mother and I thought you were wonderful, darling," but I was looking over his shoulder to the figure in the shadows, who didn't look at all out of place in her swan costume. It didn't matter what they said – and the stranger had begun nattering on about the past – because I knew beyond all doubt who my real mother was.

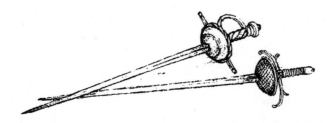

A PROPER LITTLE NOORYEFF

JEAN URE

Jamie's little sister Kim is mad on ballet, and when her teacher's short of a boy for their show, Jamie is horrifed to find himself getting roped in. The only consolation seems to be that his partner is a pretty dancer named Anita Cairncross.

THE BALLET WAS *Romeo and Juliet*, with music by Prokofiev, and according to the *Radio Times* it was going to last most of the evening – a fact which Jamie noted with the same sort of enthusiasm that he noted a period of double maths or physics scheduled for first thing on a Monday morning. He knew he was supposed to be someone who had a feeling, but the only feeling he could dredge up, as gingerly he placed himself beside Anita on a velvet sofa that looked far too fragile for actually sitting on, was the glum anticipation of boredom. If he'd known it was going to go on as long as this, he would never have come; not even to please Anita. And if he'd known it was going to be *Romeo and Juliet* – they'd been subjected to Romeo and Juliet last term, with Miss Fosdyke. It was quite the most futile play he'd ever read. Really futile. He hardly imagined that the ballet was likely to be any improvement.

147

It wasn't, to begin with. Just a load of people pratting about in fancy dress, looking like something out of a Christmas pantomime. Mrs Cairncross, glancing up from a nail-polishing session, said, "Well, it's quite pretty," but one wanted it to be more than just pretty. One wanted there to be some action. All these people in their fancy costumes were all very well, but what were they actually doing? Nothing as far as he could make out. Certainly nothing that anyone else couldn't have done. At least with Benton's Bluebells there had been some real dancing.

He found that he was disappointed, in spite of not having expected very much. He had expected it to be better than *this*. Secretly, he'd been hoping that the old Nureyev guy that everyone raved about would be so impressive that even his dad, watching back at home, would be forced to sit up and take notice. After all, the fellow must have *some*thing. Kim wasn't the only one to do her bits and pieces over him: even Anita tended to crumble at the edges. A few days ago, she'd

been showing him how to do a thing called an *entrechat* (a complicated sort of leap where you were supposed to beat your heels together in mid-air – no mean feat, as he'd discovered when he tried it). Most people, she'd said, only managed to get as far as a *six* (pronounced sees). "But as you're so good at jumping I shouldn't think you'd have too much difficulty with a *huit* (pronounced weet). Not once you've mastered the technique." A trifle jealously, since he hadn't yet mastered it sufficiently to do a *trois* or even a *deux*, let alone a *six* or a *huit*, he'd said: "What about this Nureyev, then? What can he do?" Her eyes had gone all glassy, sort of glazed over with a mist of reverence, and she'd said: "Oh, well. *Nureyev.*" (But not at all in the tones that people said oh-well-Garstin.) "I shouldn't be surprised if *he* could manage a *douze* . . ."

Whether he could or he couldn't, it didn't seem to Jamie that he was getting much of a chance to show anyone; not in *Romeo and Juliet*. He might be impressing Kim, sitting with her stubby nose glued to the box (he bet she was: he could just picture her) but Kim was so far gone he'd probably only have to scratch his left ear and she'd think he'd performed some kind of miracle. He certainly wasn't impressing anyone else. Mrs Cairncross, blowing on her nail varnish to help it dry quicker, wanted to know whether "that was the one, then . . . the one you've all got crushes on?" And when Anita didn't deign to reply: "When I was your age, it was all film stars. Tony Curtis, I remember." She gave a little laugh. "He was the one I went for." Mr Cairncross only poured himself a large bubble of brandy and said: "Nice pair of legs he's got, I'll say that for him."

It wasn't until the duel scene between Tybalt and Mercutio that things began to liven up. For the first time, Jamie found himself taking notice. This was more like it! They were going at it, hammer and tongs, all over the stage. It was one of the best sword fights he'd ever seen. He crouched forward, on the edge of his seat, tense and absorbed, watching every move – not that he didn't know the outcome, because he remembered it perfectly well from last term with Miss Fosdyke. Mercutio had always struck him as being the one decent character in the entire play: he'd been disgusted when Shakespeare had killed him off halfway through. What he was waiting for was the moment when it happened.

When it came, that moment he'd been waiting for, he was like Anita, beside him: eyes riveted, immovable. The death of Mercutio was fantastic. He didn't just lie down and die, he writhed, and rolled, and arched his back – thrashed with his limbs and curled up his muscles and bowled about the stage in hoops of agony. And yet, for all that, it was more than mere acrobatics. Watching Mercutio die he felt almost how he might feel if he were watching someone like, say, Doug. someone with whom you had had fun, who was always good for a laugh, even if at times you could cheerfully have murdered them.

He wondered which part he would rather dance, if he were to be given the choice: whether he would rather be Mercutio, who at least was a real character, even if he did get nobbled earlier on, or Romeo, who lasted longer but was such a flaming wet, mooning about all the time like some love-sick chicken. He decided he would sacrifice the length and opt for Mercutio. He wouldn't half mind playing that death scene (he made a mental note to try it out in his bedroom some time when his mum wasn't around). Of course, he would have to learn how to fence. He wondered how much lessons would cost; whether perhaps it might be a better idea to spend his savings on a fencing foil rather than the guitar he'd promised himself. If he were to buy the fencing foil—

He stiffened, sitting forward again on the edge of his seat. Now it was Romeo's turn. He was having a right go at Tybalt – obviously determined to avenge himself for the death of his friend. That was what Jamie would do, if someone had just killed Doug. He saw himself doing it (he would definitely buy that fencing foil). Maybe Romeo wasn't such a flaming wet after all. He was really putting the boot in there. He'd really got old Tybalt on the run. Any minute now—

"Got him!" Mr Cairncross reached out for his bottle of brandy. Mrs Cairncross, coming back into the room with a tray full of something or other, said: "Which one's that, then?"

"Tybalt," said Anita.

"Tibble?" said Mrs Cairncross.

Anita tightened her lips.

"*Tybalt*," she said.

"Oh! Tybalt. Wasn't he the bullying one? Jamie, have a—'

He wasn't quite sure what it was that she offered him. It sounded like "Have a canopy," but when he took one, not wanting to be thought ungracious, all it was was a bit of toast with a dob of paste smeared on it. It tasted OK, but he was terrified of dropping crumbs and found that in any case you couldn't really concentrate if you were trying to eat at the same time. Perhaps that was why Anita wouldn't have one. He could tell, from the way she frowned and shook her head, without removing her eyes from the screen, that the constant interruptions were irritating her. He bet Kim was suffering in exactly the same way at home. Mr Carr would be there in his armchair, drinking his Guinness and pretending to be watching a football match or a heavyweight title fight, every five minutes taking his nose out of his glass to shout encouragement ("Sock it to him, Rudi baby! Oh, nice one! Nice one!") while Mrs Carr would be clicking with her knitting needles, yanking strands of wool out of crackling plastic bags and looking up at all the crucial moments to ask questions. "What's happening now, then? What's he doing now? Who's been killed?"

Funny how all parents seemed to be alike. He'd have thought Anita's would be different, but obviously they were just as insensitive as everyone else's.

He swallowed his last piece of toast and sat forward, shoulder to shoulder with Anita, his elbows planted on his knees and his hands clamped either side of his head like blinkers, so that he couldn't be distracted. Having despatched the enemy, Romeo had at last come into his own. He'd really got it together now. He wasn't just mooning about any more, he really meant business. You could tell, the way they danced with each other, that he and Juliet had gone further than Jamie and Sharon had ever gone. No snatched kisses by the rabbit hutches in *Juliet's* back yard: when old Romeo had gone climbing up there to the balcony it had been for more than a good-night cuddle.

He began to revise his opinion of the great Nureyev. Maybe the fellow did have something going for him, after all. Maybe he'd been a bit too hasty, deciding that Mercutio was the part to have. Romeo's sword fight had been just as good as his, and he did still have a death scene to come. He thought that he would wait and see what the death scene was like; see whether it made up for all that mooning about at the beginning.

It certainly wasn't as spectacular as Mercutio's. Romeo didn't do acrobatics and bowl about the stage in hoops. He

died quite quietly, by the side of Juliet. In the play, Jamie had thought only what a crass idiot the man was – and had noted with relief that there was only one more page of the rubbish to go. Miss Fosdyke had asked at the end if anyone had found it sad, but no one had; not even any of the girls. When she had applied to Doug to know why not, Doug, in his usual forthright fashion, had said: "Load of cobblers, innit?" And then, when pressed to be more explicit: "Well, I mean . . . her knocking herself out with sleeping pills and him taking poison and her sticking daggers in her chest . . . bloody stupid. Not the way people carry on in real life."

He had spoken for the entire class. They had all voiced their agreement: it was bloody stupid; it wasn't the way people carried on in real life. Jamie had even added the rider that "'Fyou ask me, it ought to be done as a comedy . . . I bet that's what Shakespeare meant it for, originally. I bet if you did it as a comedy, it'd be one of the funniest things he ever wrote."

Miss Fosdyke had obligingly let them try out the death scene, with Jamie playing Juliet and Doug acting Romeo: all the class had been in stitches. Even when she'd taken them, later, to see a London production with real professional actors, it hadn't been much better. Jamie had still sat stolidly unmoved from start to finish. He didn't know what should make the ballet any different from the play – maybe it was something to do with the music, and not having to listen to all those sloppy words – but whatever it was, when Nureyev as Romeo said goodbye to Juliet for the very last time and lay down by her side to die, he felt a strange burning sensation at the back of his eyes; and when Juliet woke up and found him there, and thought at first that he was just asleep, it really started to get to him. It really did start to get to him. It was like *Ave Maria* on the organ at his great granddad's funeral when he had been the same age as Kim was now. It had done terrible things inside him so that he had wanted to blubber like a kid, even though he'd hardly known his great granddad and had actually resented having to go to the funeral in the first place because it meant missing out on a football match.

153

This flaming ballet was doing exactly the same sort of terrible things.

Mrs Cairncross picked up her empty canopy dish.

"I think I'll make some coffee," she said. She walked across to the door, passing in front of the television screen as she did so. "What time, exactly, is this thing supposed to end?"

Mr Cairncross cradled his brandy bubble.

"Any minute now, I should imagine."

"Are you going to give Jamie a lift home?"

"By all means, if he wants one."

Mrs Cairncross paused, one hand on the door knob.

"*Would* you like a lift home, Jamie?"

Hunched forward on the edge of the sofa, seeing the screen through what had now become a definite blur, Jamie pressed so hard with his fingertips against his temples that it actually hurt. He took a breath – through his mouth rather than his nose, because his nose was all blocked up and snuffly – but before he had to risk saying anything, Anita, to his immense relief, had come to his rescue.

"You might at *least* wait until it's finished."

Mrs Cairncross pulled a henpecked face.

"Sorry, I'm sure! I thought it virtually had."

"Well, it virtually *hasn't*. You haven't been watching. How can it be finished when Juliet's still alive?"

Afterwards, when Juliet had killed herself with Romeo's dagger and it really was finished and they were drinking the coffee that Mrs Cairncross had made, they asked him again, "How about this lift, then, Jamie?" but now he was ready for it, and although he still had to breathe through his mouth he was at least able to speak without making a fool of himself. He said, "It's all right, thanks. I don't mind walking," which was quite true, he didn't, but more than that he wanted to be by himself, to go over in his mind what he had just seen, to reconstruct those duel scenes before he had a chance to forget them. He didn't feel like having to make conversation, not even about cars or cricket. He rather thought that Daddy didn't feel like having to bestir himself, either, because when

Mrs Cairncross started having doubts about the Common –
"At *this* time of night? Jamie, do you think you ought?" – he
said bracingly that Jamie was a well set-up lad and that he
was quite sure he could take care of himself. "Can't you,
young man?" Anita just said: "Honestly, Mummy don't *fuss*
so. There's almost a full moon out there."

In spite of the full moon, as he was passing the wooded area
where the nutters flashed and young love went courting, he
managed to trip almost headlong over a couple of bodies
concealed in the grass. They turned out to be Marigold
Johnson and a boy from 5D, whose name he didn't know. The
boy from 5D said: "D'you mind watching where you're
treading?" Marigold Johnson just looked at him and giggled.
He muttered: "Sorry, didn't see you," and walked on,
embarrassed. It always embarrassed him when he found
people doing things like that. He only hoped to heaven that
he hadn't been making mad fencing gestures all by himself. It
would be round the school in next to no time: James Carr's
going off his rocker. Walks the Common at dead of night
making funny motions in the air . . .

He arrived home to find Kim still up, even though it was
long past her bedtime. As he climbed the stairs, he heard his
mother's voice, exasperated: "Kim, did you hear me? I said,
go to bed." And Kim's voice, somewhat petulant, in reply:
"Yes, all *right*. I'm *going*." There were sounds of feet crossly
banging their way over the sitting-room floor, then the door at
the head of the stairs was flung open and Kim flounced
through, defiant.

"*Anyway*," she said – it was obviously intended as a parting
shot – "football's only a *game*. Ballet dancers have to work *far*
harder than *foot*ballers."

"Get away with you!" That was his dad, all masculine and
jovial. "Knees bend and point your toes . . . call that work?
Load of old nannies! Wouldn't last five minutes."

Kim turned red – she looked almost as though she might be
going to burst. Jamie knew that she was wrestling with the
urge to say something rude, such as "Pig's *bum*," which was

156

the worst thing she was acquainted with just at this moment. He sympathized with her, but hoped for her sake that she managed to suppress it. After a struggle that lasted several seconds, she said: "You put one of your rotten footballers in one of Miss Tucker's classes and *he* wouldn't even last *one* minute."

"You're dead right he wouldn't!" Mr Carr chuckled. "Be too busy running for his life."

Kim opened her mouth to retort, but her mother got in first: there was a note of warning in her voice.

"If I have to tell you again—"

"Oh, all *right*," said Kim. "I'm going."

Huffily, she left the room, elbowing her way past Jamie as if he wasn't even there. They heard her stumping up the stairs and along the passage overhead.

"You shouldn't tease her like that," said Mrs Carr. "It's not fair."

"Go on!" Mr Carr grinned, unrepentant. "Load of old nannies, the lot of 'em." He winked at Jamie across the room. "Where've you been, then? Out on the razzle?"

"Been out with Doug," said Jamie. He didn't quite know why he said it, except that he wasn't in a mood for having his leg pulled, and if he said "round at Anita's" his dad would never be able to resist the temptation. "Went down the disco. Down Bell Street."

He only hoped Doug wouldn't ask him, Monday morning, why he *hadn't* been down the disco, down Bell Street. He had a sneaking sort of feeling, which he tried hard to suppress, that it was where he ought to have been.

AND OLLY DID TOO

JAMILA GAVIN

J ENNY SAID, "When I grow up, I'm going to be a ballet dancer."

Her younger brother Olly said, "I will too," but everyone laughed and took no notice.

Jenny tried to look like a ballet dancer. She always wore her hair swept tightly back into a bun; she always stood with a very straight back; she always held her head up high to show off her long neck; and when she walked, she turned her feet out, just like ballet dancers do.

Olly rushed about like a wild thing, wearing his track suit and trainers. He kept jumping and leaping and kicking his legs in the air, like a frisky horse.

"Are you trying to be a footballer, Olly?" people asked.

"No," said Olly, "I'm going to be a ballet dancer!" Everyone roared with laughter, because Olly was such a little toughie with his spiky hair and rough and tumbling body.

Every Wednesday after school, Mum took Jenny to her ballet lesson. Olly went too, but only to watch because Mum couldn't leave him at home on his own.

Olly used to fidget. He watched Jenny in her black leotard

and pink, fluffy, cross-over cardigan. He kicked his feet against the chair while she put on her shining pink ballet shoes and crisscrossed the pink satin ribbons round her ankles.

Mum had to rap Olly across the knees and tell him to keep still. In the end, she would send him right away to the back of the hall with a box of action toys, to keep him out of mischief. But as soon as the piano started thumping out the tunes for the dancers to do their exercises, Olly did them too where no one could see him.

Every day, Jenny practised her ballet movements in the kitchen. She would hold the back of a chair and then call out the French words for each position:

"Première position . . . pliéz jettez . . . attitude . . ."

Olly did too. He pointed his toes and bent his knees and lifted his leg forwards and backwards; he raised his arm and curved his hands and always remembered to look in whatever direction his fingers went. But nobody noticed. They thought he was fooling about.

Having a ballet dancer in the family was such hard work. There always seemed to be a show to rehearse or an exam to prepare. Father couldn't count the number of times he had driven Jenny to and from draughty church halls; and Mother couldn't remember how many costumes she'd made. Olly had never known a time when the house wasn't scattered with bits of stiff net for tutus, satin and silks for bodices and ribbons, or when every surface wasn't covered with boxes of pins and buttons and sequins.

Olly liked dressing up too, but everyone thought he was just messing around. He would grab the old green velvet curtains Mum had kept by for cutting up, and swing them round his shoulders like a cloak; and how everybody laughed when he put on his mother's black leather boots which almost went up to his thighs.

"What on earth do you think you look like in those!" exclaimed Jenny, scornfully.

"That's what princes wear, isn't it?" retorted Olly.

When it was Jenny's birthday, they took her to the ballet. Olly went too, because Granny couldn't babysit that night. Everyone thought Olly would hate going to the theatre and they hoped he wouldn't wriggle and keep asking to go to the toilet. Mum said he would probably be bored and fall asleep.

When they arrived at the theatre, there were lots and lots of girls wearing velvet dresses with broad sashes. All had their hair swept under Alice-bands or twisted into net buns; and all were standing like swans, holding their heads up very high and with their feet turned out. There were many boys too, trying to look grand and grown-up, but Olly didn't notice. He couldn't stand still long enough to notice. He was so excited. He couldn't wait to get inside and see the dancers.

"One day," whispered Mum proudly to Jenny, "everyone will be queueing to see you!"

Olly said, "Will they come and see me too?" But everyone laughed.

They went in through the glass doors into the foyer with the red velvet plush carpet. Those who hadn't already bought tickets were queueing hopefully, while others, like Dad, fumbled in jackets and pockets for theirs.

"You're in the upper circle," said a man in black and white evening dress examining their tickets. "You take the left staircase."

Jenny walked sedately up the stairs, sliding her hand along the gold banister like a princess. She didn't look to the right or the left, but straight ahead, as though a handsome prince was waiting for her at the top.

Olly hopped and jumped and would have raced up two at a time if his legs had been long enough. He couldn't wait to get inside.

"Hurry up, Jenny!" he begged.

"Behave yourself, Olly. We're going to the ballet, not a football match," said Mum sternly.

At last they were inside. At last they found their seats. They were rather high up, but had a perfect view right down to the stage. Dad turned, to warn Olly to sit still and not to dare

make a noise, but he didn't need to. Olly was leaning forward watching the musicians coming into the dark orchestral pit below the stage. First the harpist came in, because he took the longest to tune all those strings; then came a horn player, because she wanted to practise a difficult bit; and one by one, the violinist and cellists, the clarinetists and flautists and all the other players came in with their instruments.

The leader of the orchestra entered with his violin under his arm. The audience clapped and when he had bowed and sat down, the oboist played an A and all the players tuned into it.

Finally, the conductor made his entrance. He climbed up on to a rostrum and bowed to the audience while everybody clapped. Then the conductor faced his players.

The lights went down. There was a huge hush, and with a wave of a baton the music started. The great, heavy curtain rose slowly upwards.

Olly never moved a muscle; he might have been a statue, his body was so still, and his eyes so fixed. But his soul heaved like an ocean. His spirit flew like a bird. It soared across the darkened auditorium; it wafted among the white, billowing skirts of the girls, and sprang up, up, up with the shining princes in their glittering jackets. The dancers no longer seemed to be ordinary human beings, but enchanted people; magic people; the way their bodies created changing shapes and patterns, sometimes moving like one body; arms lifting and falling, legs bending and stretching, backs arching and heads turning, all at the same time. And the way the stage was no longer just a wooden stage, but in one scene it was brilliantly lit as a magnificent royal palace, and in the next, it was a dark, menacing forest. If it was real, then Olly wanted to be up there with them, dancing and leaping to the lilting rhythms of the music; but if it was a dream, and it seemed to be a dream, then he never never never wanted to wake up.

After that, Olly was always dreaming; day dreams and night dreams. Sometimes he dreamed in school, when he should have been doing his sums, but instead, he found himself floating up to the ceiling. Suddenly he was astride a black horse and galloping across a night sky; a bejewelled turban of silk was wound round his head, and a cloak of darkness whirled behind him. Then he was a hunter, stalking through a forest hung with diamonds and pearls, where long-legged spiders spun webs of silver, and strange-winged gnomes sprang through the air. Sometimes he was a magician or a king, or simply just a dancer spinning through space.

Most of all, he dreamt he was up on that stage, where the lights glittered above him like stars; where he could hear the squeak of the ballet shoes as the dancers pirouetted and twirled, the swish of costumes and the clouds of music which rose from the pit below, flowing into his arms and legs.

One day, Mum and Dad took Jenny to an audition. It was to choose the best dancers to go to a special ballet school. Jenny didn't really want to go because it meant she would have to miss her riding lesson. All of a sudden, Jenny had become mad about horses, and wasn't so sure now that she wanted to be a dancer.

"Of course you must go, Jenny," said Mother with a frown. "You've always wanted to be a ballet dancer, and this may be your one big chance."

Olly went too, because he couldn't be left on his own.

An ancient lady, who looked about a hundred years old, leant her chin on a silver-tipped cane and watched every child with the eye of a hawk. Olly had been told to sit quietly at the back, but though he was quiet, he couldn't sit still. When the children were told to stand, he stood; when they were told to walk, he walked; he walked just as the princes had walked that day at the ballet, with heads held proudly and one arm lifted out before him, making a noble gesture.

He walked down the side aisle, until he was nearly at the front. Nobody had noticed, because all eyes were fixed on the children who were auditioning – except the old lady. Somehow, she noticed. Perhaps she had eyes at the back of her head. Perhaps she was a witch, and her back tingled when somebody danced. She seemed to see everything, though no one knew. Suddenly she got up – or did she spring? For as she got to her feet, she was no longer just an old lady, she was a dancer. Olly stopped, and shrank, watching, into the shadows.

She walked along the line of children, pointing with her silver cane. She studied their fronts and their backs; their thighs and their legs; their knees and their ankles, and she even made them walk barefoot, so that she could examine their toes.

"You may have to look as delicate as flowers, but you have to be as strong as tigers," she muttered.

"I'm strong!" exclaimed Olly, suddenly stepping out boldly before her.

"Olly!" hissed his mother, very shocked. "Don't be rude. Go and play with your cars at the back of the hall."

But the old, old lady waved her silver cane at him.

"Yes, I've been watching you. Let me have a look at you, my boy. Strip off down to your underpants."

Some children giggled, but Olly did as he was asked.

"Walk across the stage!" she ordered. Olly walked.

"Point your toes, bend your knees, stand on one leg, jump in the air." Olly did all those things.

About fifty children had come to the audition that day, but they knew that only six could be chosen. At the end of every session, a person with a large notebook would say to the parents of each child, "We'll let you know."

So they had to go home and wait. They waited and waited. Mum was longing to know whether Jenny had been chosen, and watched for the post every day. But Jenny hardly noticed the time going by. She was clamouring for a pair of riding boots and jodhpurs and she was asking if she could go to pony camp in the summer.

At last, one day, a letter came through the door. It was from the ballet school. Mother opened it with trembling fingers.

"Well," exclaimed Dad with breathless impatience, "has Jenny got in?"

Mum didn't answer. She read the letter once, then she read it again.

"For goodness sake, tell me!" begged Dad. "What do they say?"

Finally, Mum replied in a small voice, "They say they want Olly!"

"Oh, good!" yelled Olly, leaping into the air. "I always wanted to be a dancer!"

"Does that mean I don't have to go to ballet classes any more?" cried Jenny with a grin. "Oh good!" I'd much rather go horse-riding instead!"

Olly shut his eyes tight. He imagined himself up on the stage. He could feel the warmth of the lights and the smell of the face paints; he could hear the music casting its spell over him, so that his feet began to twitch. Before him was a wide, empty space. With a whoop of joy, he gave a giant leap. With his arms and legs outstretched, he was like a tiger in full flight.

That year, a specially chosen group of children went to the ballet school to train as dancers. Olly went too.

GRACE

HARRIET CASTOR

"**D**O YOU THINK," Lizzie said to me one day (Mrs Barker had gone off to get some textbooks from the staffroom and we were supposed to be working through page 73 on our own), "– do you think – that your name affects what sort of person you are?"

"Don't tell me – you're about to develop some royalty fixation and start keeping corgis?" I said.

"No, stupid. Like—" She chewed on the end of her biro and looked into the middle distance thoughtfully, "Like – would I have been the same person if I'd been called Stacey, or – Ermintrude?"

"Ermintrude?" I scrunched up my nose. "Definitely not. If you really had to spend your life being called after a pink cow in *The Magic Roundabout* it would definitely get to you. I think you might manage a couple of years of playgroup . . . you never know, you might even get past a term or two of infants school – but then you'd definitely go stark raving bonkers."

At this point Mrs Barker came back in and asked me in a loud annoyed voice which question I'd got to. Since I hadn't even read the first one yet, that shut me up for a bit.

"Anyway, look at me—" I said later on, at break.

Lizzie did. "Yeah?"

"No – I mean, take me as an example. Can you think of anyone in the whole world who fits their name less than I do?"

"You have a point."

And so I did. My name, you see, is Grace. Grace Castleman Sams, to give you the full caboodle. Castleman is my mum's maiden name, so there's an excuse for that – but Grace? Sometimes I look at my parents and wonder what on earth they were thinking of at my christening when the vicar asked, "And her name is . . . ?"

They must have been able to tell even at that age that I was going to be the *least* graceful person the world has ever known. Mum says I was even the wrong way round inside her when it was time for me to be born, so that should have given her a clue.

But I gave up trying to figure my mum out long ago.

"You're late, Grace," was the first thing she said to me that afternoon when I got back from school.

"I know, I know, I know," I said, storming down the hall so that my schoolbag clattered along the banister rails, and flopping into a kitchen chair.

"Have you got your dance bag packed?" She'd followed me into the kitchen, and now flicked back the cuff of her jacket and tapped at her watch.

Without getting up, I reached for the fridge handle (that's one of the advantages of having long arms). "Well . . ." Reaching the other way, I got a glass off the draining board and slopped some milk into it. "Not *exactly*."

"You know how Mr Festenstein hates you to be late—"

"I know—"

"And you should at least make an effort for the first class of term—"

"I'm going, I'm going!" I slammed the empty glass back on the table, and wiped my mouth with the back of my hand like they do in cowboy movies (Mum hates me doing that; she

167

doesn't understand that it's an artistic *reference*). Then I skidded back down the hall and took the stairs three at a time.

"Grace!" The whole house was shaking.

"Sorry!"

Mr Festenstein's one of life's originals. He's pretty old – sixty-something, I reckon. His hair's white, anyway, though his eyes are really clear and he's only a bit wrinkly. When you see him in lessons he's always wearing the same clothes: a faded red velvet jacket, a crisp white shirt and a purple silk cravat. He has these loose white trousers like you'd imagine people wearing to summer yacht parties fifty years ago. And they're always absolutely spotless (if anyone ever wanted to make a soap powder commercial they should go to him for the "after" picture). On his feet, he wears weird canvas pumps – really soft ones, so that he can point his toes when he's demonstrating steps.

"Ah, Miss Sams!" That night he greeted me in ringing tones from the far end of the room.

"S-sorry I'm late," I panted, then promptly fell over. I'd tied one of my shoe ribbons badly and it'd just unwound itself and tripped me up. Everyone else in the class – already standing at the *barre* – turned round to look and giggled.

"Class, class!" Mr Festenstein clapped his hands. "Grace is not a cabaret. Let us mark through that *plié* exercise once more for her benefit. And!"

I scrambled to my feet – ribbon re-tied – and dived for my place at the back of the *barre*. I always stand at the back. It's not just shyness; if I stood in front of anyone, Mr Festenstein wouldn't be able to see them.

"*Grand plié* – one, two; come up – three, four; forward bend – five, six, seven—"

As I wafted down towards my feet I wished for the zillionth time that they were smaller; my ballet shoes are so large they look like great floppy pitta breads. In fact I spend most of my time in every ballet lesson wishing: wishing I could float

round on my pointes like a gossamer wispy thing, or turn a pirouette without falling over, or jump in the air and not make a noise like a herd of wildebeest when I land. But I'm a realist; face facts, I say. And fact number one is this: I'm not cut out to be a ballerina. Never have been, and never will be.

On the way out to the car after class, I tried to tackle Mum about it. It wasn't the first time, and I knew it would be useless.

"Honestly, Mum. It's not that I don't like ballet – I do. Watching it is great. But *doing* it . . . I'm a born loser in a leotard. It's a waste of time – and money." (I thought this was crafty; Mum's always saving the pennies.)

"You have no tenacity." Mum frowned as she held out her keys and beeped the car alarm off. "A lot of girls would be grateful to have lessons with such a wonderful teacher. And you're still slouching horribly—" She grabbed my shoulders and yanked them back like I was some sergeant on parade.

"I'm only slouching because I'm miserable, and I'm only miserable because I have to go to ballet!" I cried, as she walked round to the driver's side.

Mum tutted in irritation and opened the car door. "Don't be melodramatic."

"You know what I reckon?" said Lizzie the next day, prodding her cheese pie absent-mindedly.

"Go on, stun me."

"I reckon—" Lizzie leant towards me, so her school tie flolloped into her dinner. "I reckon it's your mum's own *thwarted ambition* that's behind it all."

"You what? You're making her sound like Lady Macbeth!"

"Well—" Lizzie looked down and started scraping the cheese pie back onto her plate. "You told me she wanted to be a ballerina when she was little, didn't you?"

I resisted the temptation to say, "Who, Lady Macbeth?" and said instead, "OK, that's true. But Dad always says he wanted to be a spaceman when he was little, and you don't catch him packing me off to NASA for astronaut lessons do you?"

Lizzie shrugged. "Just a thought."

It *was* a thought, and the more I turned it over in my mind, the more it made sense. Mum *had* said she'd longed to go to ballet lessons when she was little, but that Gran and Grandad just hadn't been able to afford it. She'd told me once, almost tearfully, of how she'd missed her chance of doing the one thing she'd set her heart on. And you could tell, just from looking at Mum, that she probably would have been really good at ballet too. She's not all stretched out and gangly like Dad and me; instead, she's really dainty, with slim legs and tiny feet and a dead straight back. She stands and sits so straight and proud you'd think she'd had a broom-handle sewn into the back of her dress. And she's got this beautiful poised head on a slim neck, like the stem of a really fine wine goblet. In fact, we're so different, that if you saw us together in the street you'd never guess in a million years that we're related.

Anyhow, as that week went by, and another humiliating

ballet lesson loomed, this thought of Lizzie's turned itself into an idea. I knew I couldn't just come out with it to Mum, or she'd tell me I was being silly. But it seemed like the perfect answer: for me and for Mum. So I decided I'd have to use a bit of cunning.

When Wednesday night came round again, I made sure I was a little early for class, so I'd have time to study the notice board outside the studio before I went in. I even took a pad and pencil with me and noted something down.

"What you doing?" said Imelda Potts, one of the girls in my ballet class who just *has* to be the nosiest person in the world.

"Never you mind," I said. I smiled a secretive smile at her and put my notepad back in my bag.

She stared at me, too, as she was gathering her belongings after class and saw me go up to Mr Festenstein for a private word. But I let her stare.

I had a plan.

"Dad?"

"Hmmm?"

Dad had his nose in a very large, boring-looking book. He was lying on the floor in the sitting room, which he always does when he's reading; he says it's really difficult to find chairs that are comfortable when you're six foot seven. I plumped down beside him.

"Dad?" I flicked the cover of the book with my finger. He put it down on his chest.

"What, O Annoying One?"

"You know Mum's tracksuit? The lilac velour one?"

"Yeees?" Dad said cautiously.

"Do you think you can get Mum to wear it next Tuesday? You know, in the morning you could say – "Ooh, I haven't seen you wearing that in a long time and it's so nice," sort of thing?"

"May I ask why?"

I thought about it. "No," I said at last. "Sorry."

"No to you too, then," said Dad amiably, and the book went

back up round his face like a fireguard.

"Oh, all right." The book came down again, and I leant over and whispered in Dad's ear. It took quite a while to explain. But finally I straightened up and looked at him with my strictest Mrs Barker face. "You mustn't tell a soul, though."

"Dib, dib, dib," said Dad obediently, holding up three of his great sausagy fingers. "Scout's honour."

"Are you sure you heard Mr Festenstein correctly?" asked Mum later the same evening, puzzling over the diary.

"Absolutely." I nodded vigorously. "It's some . . . er . . . conference he has to go to on Wednesday. Some ballet teachers' thing."

"So you're only moving to Tuesday for this week?"

"That's right. He's putting us together with his usual Tuesday night class."

Mum shook her head slightly and made a note. "I wonder if he'll give a reduction for that," she muttered.

From behind, Dad winked at me. I was so desperate not to laugh I had to go and rattle loudly in the cutlery drawer.

"That's right – set the table, Grace, there's a good girl."

When Tuesday came round I was a bit nervous. The first hurdle was hoping Dad would get through his bit of the plan without messing up. Mum came down to breakfast still in her dressing gown. "Your father certainly is in a strange mood today," she said, then pointed at me. "Elbows off the table."

She reached above me and started rooting through the airing cupboard. When she finally brought out the lilac track-suit, I breathed a sigh of relief. I was about to say, "Oh, I haven't seen that for ages! It's ace!" when I remembered – just in the nick of time – that I always used to tease Mum about that tracksuit. I stuffed the last corner of toast into my mouth instead and concentrated on chewing.

The day passed edgily. I must have looked at the clock on our classroom wall at least once every five minutes. But when the final bell rang, I was ready. I sprang up from my seat and would have been first out of the room if I hadn't caught my sleeve on the doorhandle.

"Ouf!" said Lizzie as I cannoned back into her.

"Sorry!" I shouted, detaching myself and pelting down the corridor. "Must dash!"

When I got home, Mum was in the kitchen, so I dashed straight upstairs. I kicked off my shoes before tiptoeing into her and Dad's bedroom and clicking open the wardrobe door as softly as I could. I hardly dared breathe; I was listening out, like a cat-burglar, for a footstep on the stairs. But there was nothing. All clear.

Two minutes later, I clicked the wardrobe door shut again and, clutching the carrier bag with my booty inside it, I made it back into my own room. Then I started banging about again like normal, just so that Mum wouldn't get suspicious.

"Grace!"

"Sorry!"

Mum parked the car, with the engine still running. I said, "Can you come in with me? I – I'm not quite sure what time we finish tonight."

Mum frowned. "Won't it be an hour, as usual?"

"Well—" I grimaced out at the twilight. "Since Mr Festenstein's putting two classes together, it might be a bit longer."

Mum sighed, turned the key and pulled it out of the ignition. "Come on, then," she said wearily.

My heart was really thumping in my chest now. Would my plan come off? Would Mr Festenstein remember?

I pushed through the community centre's front door ahead of Mum. In the little hallway, which doubles up as a rather drafty changing room for those people who don't like changing in the loos (which is most of us), there were quite a few women standing about, some youngish and some older, and one man too, in the far corner, wearing a banana-yellow sweatshirt.

Mum checked her watch. "Did you get the time right,

Grace? These must be parents waiting. Either we're early or your class has already gone in—"

I was just wondering how to answer that when Mr Festenstein made a grand entrance through the studio door. "Good evening, people!" he declared jovially. "Come along in!"

The women and the one man, tweaking at their leggings and tracksuits, and hopping as they put on their ballet shoes, made their way towards the door. Mr Festenstein then spied Mum, and flung his arms out flamboyantly.

"And Mrs Sams! What a pleasure it is to welcome you to my adult class!"

Mum looked utterly confused – "gobsmacked", Lizzie would have said.

"Adult class? But – I'm just bringing Grace—" she spluttered.

"No, no!" Mr Festenstein waggled a finger from side to side like a metronome. "It is you I am teaching this evening, Mrs Sams. We start in two minutes!"

Mum turned back to me, her face clouding over. But I immediately delved in my bag and whipped out the pair of her jazz shoes I'd taken from her wardrobe earlier.

"These'll do fine while you haven't any proper ballet shoes," I gabbled. "And your tracksuit's perfect too."

"Come along, dear lady!" Mr Festenstein held both hands out towards her.

"I – I couldn't possibly. I'm forty-three and I've never had a ballet lesson in my life!"

Mr Festenstein looked at Mum steadily. "Then we haven't a moment to lose, Mrs Sams." He looked so serious Mum didn't know what to say next, and before she knew it she was being ushered into the studio. As he shut the door behind them both, Mr Festenstein winked at me through the porthole window. I grinned back, but my stomach was tying itself in knots. What had I done? Would Mum be furious with me when she came out?

The hour dragged by as if it had been three. I'd brought a book, but I couldn't settle to reading it – I gazed numbly at the noticeboard instead, though after the whole hour I couldn't have told you a single thing that was pinned there. Then at last the swing door thumped back and the class came out. Mum emerged last of all, and Mr Festenstein was right behind her.

"She's a natural," he said, steering her towards me by the shoulders as if she was about *six* and *I* was her mother. "Turn-out to die for and the most exquisite feet. Bring her back next week, will you?"

I laughed. "I'll do my best!"

Mum was looking flushed and still rather confused. But pleased – very pleased.

"Did you like it?" I whispered when Mr Festenstein had turned away and Mum was pulling on her coat.

Mum looked at me sharply. "It was brilliant. I loved every minute. And you, my girl –" She jabbed at my shoulder with her finger, "– set me up something rotten!"

"Sometimes . . ." I said, giving her my best Clint Eastwood tough guy stare, "a girl's gotta do what a girl's gotta do."

That was all a few weeks ago now. I stopped my ballet lessons right then and there. Mum finally did wake up to the fact that there was only one person cut out for ballet in our family . . . and it wasn't *me*. Now I've started at the Drama Club on Saturday mornings instead, and I really like it.

Mum, on the other hand, hasn't missed a single Tuesday night at the community centre. She'd move mountains to get there. She's even bought a proper leotard and ballet shoes. And at the end of term, Mr Festenstein says, I'll be able to sit in for a class and see how she's doing.

I have this hunch I'm going to feel really proud of her.

I can't wait.

THE TROUBLE WITH
SALVATORE

RUMER GODDEN

from Listen to the Nightingale

Lottie is a boarder at the famous ballet school, Queen's Chase.

"SALVATORE RUFFINO," said Mrs Challoner, "is a most disruptive boy."

"He seems to want to be diabolical," said Polly Walsh. Nothing seemed to delight Salvatore more than spoiling any kind of peace: if two boys were playing chess he would come quietly and upset the board; if anyone were painting, he would knock the water over the picture. He put salt in the sugar bowls on the dining tables and, knowing Mrs Merry's dread of mice, he brought three dead ones back from home at the weekend – there were plenty of mice in Soho – and put them on a plate in the refrigerator for her to find.

"Another of Salvatore's stupid jokes," said Lottie loftily.

"But why?" asked Mrs Challoner. "They all love Mrs Merry."

"I think he has some grudge against the world," said Polly Walsh. "Also he wants to make his mark with the other boys."

"He goes the worst way about it."

The boys had disliked him from the first: it was his luscious

177

good looks, his boasting, especially about his papa.

"Who's your papa?" he asked Desmond.

"Lord Cherston," said Desmond whose father happened to be an earl. Salvatore was unabashed.

"Bet he hasn't a car-hire business with a hundred cars and a restaurant and a delicatessen."

"You were a silly to tell them that," Polly told him, and sure enough the children were soon calling him Macaroni and Pasta Pest. Pest was right, yet he intrigued them.

To begin with, the way he had got himself to Queen's Chase was as unbelievable to the other children as it had been to Lottie. "You mean you never had a dancing lesson until now?" said Desmond.

"Never," said Salvatore. "I used to go to a day school near the Theatre Royal and often some of our boys took part in an opera or ballet when children were needed who didn't have to dance or sing, just act a little. Then *The Dream* was put on" – *The Dream* was a ballet taken from *A Midsummer Night's Dream* – and as always a boy was needed for the Indian changeling. "I'm so dark I could be an Indian and so small and light I could be a fairy changeling – see how light I am," and Salvatore did a leap, inordinately high and landed without a sound, "so they chose me. Ennis Glyn was dancing Titania, Yuri Koszorz Oberon. Oberon had to throw me across the stage." As he told this Salvatore changed before their eyes into an intensely earnest boy who said, "It was then that I knew I would be a dancer."

"And they took you! Why?"

"Because I have such talent."

"Oh dear! Saying that's not going to do him any good," said Polly.

The second-year boys had already noted that Mr Max, who did not usually teach the smallest boys – he was the senior ballet master – now visited the first-year boys' class far more often then he had done in their time and, "It's aeons since I had a boy like this," Desmond heard Miss McKenzie say.

What the children found strangest of all was that Salvatore

did not seem to care in the least that he was unpopular. "Nobody likes you," Priscilla told him. Salvatore shrugged and whistled as if to say, "I like myself." He led a blithe life of his own on which it seemed no one made any impression. When Mr Ormond lost patience with him, which he seldom did with any of the boys, on the evening of the day he gave Salvatore his worst scolding and punishment – "No sweets or comics for two weeks" – Polly caught him making Mr Ormond an apple-pie bed.

"I could hardly keep a straight face," Polly told Mrs Challoner, "I must say I've longed sometimes to make Mr Ormond an apple-pie bed. And it *is* hard for him." Polly meant Salvatore not Mr Ormond. "If you've been spoiled it isn't easy to get unspoiled."

"Yes, look at Irene St Charles," said Mrs Challoner.

Discipline at Queen's Chase was strict. "It has to be or the children could never get through what they have to do," said Mrs Challoner, "which is to work twice as hard as children in ordinary schools."

Salvatore, it seemed, had never had any discipline and, "I don't like the hours," he explained to Mrs Challoner.

He hated being woken by the bell and having to get up at once, otherwise Desmond who was monitor in the dormitory pulled the bedclothes off him.

"Make my own bed?" Salvatore had asked in astonishment.

"Well, who do you think will do it for you?" asked Polly. "If you're going to be a dancer you'll have to do everything for yourself." That aspect of dancing had not occurred to Salvatore.

"Timetables mean you have to be on time," Mr Ormond told him. Salvatore could not get used to that. "Late again!" said one school teacher after another – he was never late for dancing, Mrs Challoner noted.

"Go back to the end of the queue, you little twerp," a big boy would order as Salvatore tried to edge in front of the long line of boys and girls waiting with their trays for lunch; it had not occurred to the big boy that Salvatore had never stood in a queue before.

Worst of all was night time. "*Bed at half past eight! Lights out at nine!* But . . . that's just the time when I used to go out," he cried in dismay.

"Out!" The others stared.

It was Polly who discovered that, at home, when Mr Ruffino and Serafina thought Salvatore was in bed, he used to creep out leaving a dummy pillow figure, escape through a bathroom window and down the fire escape to wander in the streets. "Those streets!" said Polly with a shudder. "God knows what he saw and learned."

Jake and some of the big boys encouraged Salvatore to tell. Salvatore was flattered and, "I expect he makes it highly lurid," said Mr Ormond wearily. He could tell ghost stories too, terrifying the younger boys, especially the youngest, Thomas.

"You know that dark place in the hall just outside the Salon," Salvatore would begin, "and the big mirror that hangs there? If you went at midnight and looked into it, the mirror would crack from side to side and blood would come out." Salvatore's eyes glistened. The term was getting on for winter and by half past four, one of the times of Thomas's dancing class, the hall was dark. Thomas had to pass the mirror and shook with fear.

"Don't be thick," Desmond said. "Ask Mr Salvatore why the mirror isn't cracked in the morning and who mopped up the blood?"

"It's *supernatural*," said Salvatore, making that a fearsome word.

Polly could have told that Salvatore could be frightened too. He did not like the wide spaces of the Park, especially after dark and at night lay awake, "Listening to the dark," she said. The first time he heard an owl hoot he was out of bed and into Polly's room trembling.

"It's a ghost. It says, "Who? Who? Who did that? Who did this?" That's always me. Oh, Polly" – he always called her Polly – "oh, Polly, does it mean I'm going to die? *Die!*" No one would have recognised the hard little braggart of the day.

"He's impervious," Mr Ormond said in despair.

"The imp part is right," Polly agreed. "I think it will always be there but you mean he doesn't feel. It may astonish you, but I think Salvatore feels more deeply than almost any of the boys. That's why he behaves as he does. He knows he's a misfit."

"Except for dancing." Mrs Challoner said it thoughtfully.

Salvatore unwisely started baiting the girls; he fastened Sybil's plaits to the back of her chair with a drawing pin while she was eating. Salvatore was deft-fingered; the drawing pin came out but the jerk to her plaits hurt when Sybil got up. He put gravel in their house shoes while they were dancing, and another of his jokes, a snake this time, in Anne-Marie's locker. He offered them chocolates made of *papier-mâché* but he always excepted Lottie though he made her a special target, courting her in a stately Italian way that embarrassed her acutely. "Pasta Pest," she hissed. He even invaded the girls' table at meals to try to sit next to her and on Saturday morning's folk dancing – the only time boys and girls danced together – when it was time for the *grande promenade*, he would dash across the room and seize her. Usually she managed to free herself but once Mr Belton who took the class, commanded, "Charlotte, you and Priscilla dance with Salvatore," and they were arm in arm. Lottie had to admit that promenading with Salvatore was different from doing it with any other boy; there was a verve and dash about him which was infectious but at the end he laughed as he let her go. "You liked that, didn't you?"

"I hated it," said Lottie.

"I think Salvatore's keen on you," Irene told her, not without envy.

"He isn't," said Lottie fiercely. "I won't have it."

"Why won't you leave Charlotte alone?" said Irene.

The first-year girls were waiting for their weekly class with Miss McKenzie when Salvatore, who should not have been anywhere near, came butting in. "Leave her alone," said Irene.

He surveyed them. "You're all jealous."

"Jealous?"

"Yes, because she's the best dancer among you lot. That's why I chose her."

"*Chose me!*" Lottie nearly choked. But Irene was crimson with indignation. She gave Salvatore a slap across the face.

Salvatore leapt at her but even he, strong as he was, had no chance against ten girls. In a minute they had him on the ground, two of them knelt on him pummelling him. Anne-Marie and Sybil held his legs and pinched them; Priscilla pulled his jersey over his head. Lottie stood aghast, too horrified to join in.

It might have turned more vicious but Miss McKenzie came to take the class. "*Girls!* What *are* you doing? Get up at once. At *once*. Have you completely forgotten where you are?"

Panting but triumphant they got up leaving Salvatore on the floor.

"And you?" said Miss McKenzie to him. "What are you doing here? No," to the girls, "I don't want to hear any tales," and to Salvatore, "Go back where you should be. I shall report this to Mr Ormond."

Salvatore stood up, pulling his jersey down; flushed and dishevelled, he had red marks on his face and neck and legs, his hair had fallen over his eyes; he was furious. "Just you wait," he told the girls and, "Just *you* wait," he said to Miss McKenzie.

Next week the girls came to get their shoes for Miss McKenzie's class. They kept them in linen bags in pigeon holes in the changing room: their soft dancing shoes, heeled ones for character dancing and their new precious pale pink satin *pointe* shoes, which they had meticulously darned under Mamzelly's watchful eyes and sewn on ribbons.

They stopped; none of the left-foot *pointe* shoes were there – except Lottie's.

"If only he had taken mine too," mourned Lottie. It made her feel horridly conspicuous.

"Only the *left* shoes?" asked Mrs Challoner and had to say, "One has to admit it's a neat revenge." All the girls' ballet teachers gathered when Mrs Challoner sent for Salvatore.

"Salvatore, where did you put them?"

"Threw them in the pond," said Salvatore sweetly.

"*Mon Dieu!*" screamed Mamzelly.

"I don't believe that for a moment," said Mrs Challoner. And, "Mr Ruffino," she told Salvatore's papa who had been summoned, "that boy held out against all of us grown-ups. It wasn't until evening that his matron, Miss Walsh, found the shoes in a pillow case under the pillow in his bed." Mrs Challoner had to say too, "Mr Ruffino, there has been trouble ever since Salvatore came."

"You mean Salvatore, my Salvatore, did all these things?"

"Didn't he do them at his other school?"

"Nobody told me." Mr Ruffino passed his hand over what was left of his hair as if he were bewildered. "It is so difficult," he told Mrs Challoner. "Children without a mother and I am not a young father when it might be easier to understand. Serafina, my housekeeper, spoils them, and I so busy with the shop and restaurant, the car business. I try, but Salvatore, he does not seem to care."

"I think there is one way of making Salvatore care," said Mrs Challoner, "Suspend him from dancing."

"If I had my way he would be expelled," said Mr Ormond. "He's nothing but a nuisance."

"Nothing!" For once Miss McKenzie was shrill, "I've told you I haven't had a boy of such promise for years."

"Just because the brat is good at dancing."

"May I remind you the reason he is here is his dancing—"

Mrs Challoner intervened. "All the same, he must behave. I'm sure Ennis would agree?"

Ennis Glyn saw Salvatore herself.

"You mean I'm not to dance!" Salvatore could not believe his ears.

"Why should you dance?" asked Ennis Glyn. "You show no respect for other dancers – or for their property." She tried not to let her lips twitch when she thought of the left shoes. "So you will be suspended from all dancing for a fortnight."

"It should be a month," Mrs Challoner had said.

But again Miss McKenzie had cried, "Oh no!"

"A fortnight," said Ennis Glyn.

"Two whole weeks!"

"As far as we are concerned it might have been for ever. I was going to ask your father to take you away."

"For a few little mistakes?" Salvatore was shocked.

"Added up they are not little. You have shown yourself to be disruptive, without respect for people and property. If it happens once again, Salvatore, that will be the end of your time with us." Miss Glyn spoke very seriously. "As it is you are lucky it's only two weeks."

Salvatore was appalled. "What shall I do?" he asked piteously.

"*Try* and behave. Also, you will apologise to each of those girls," and the great Ennis Glyn asked, "Why did you except Charlotte Tew?"

To her surprise Salvatore blushed.

MAYBE NEXT YEAR . . .

AMY HEST

Kate lives in Manhatten with her sister, Pinky, their grandmother and old Mr Schumacher. Kate loves ballet, and she and her best friend Peter are due to audition for the National Ballet School.

IT'S HARD TO BELIEVE how things change in our house from one day to the next. On Monday Nana and Mr Schumacher take a long subway ride to Queens. They don't get home until after dark, happily reporting they have just bought nearly one hundred pounds of flour and butter, sugar, eggs, and chocolate.

"A hundred pounds!" I shriek.

"We got everything wholesale," Mr Schumacher says.

"If we buy in bulk," Nana explains, "it's a lot cheaper." She ties an apron – the one with yellow chickens on the pockets – around her waist. "Dinner will be late," she apologizes.

"When do we start baking?" asks Pinky.

"Mr Klein, the man who sold us the ingredients, guarantees a delivery tomorrow," answers Mr Schumacher. "He gave his word that his trucks are moving despite the snowstorm."

"How many cookies will we bake, to start?" I ask.

I must admit I'm getting awfully excited about Mr

Schumacher's new business. Imagine having a cookie factory right in your own apartment! Mr Schumacher will get rich. Maybe he'll even be rich enough to keep me in those expensive toe shoes. That way Nana can't complain that my dancing is unaffordable. Maybe he'll even be rich enough to take me to the ballet once in a while . . . and of course, he won't be feeling useless and old.

After a picnic-style dinner of salami sandwiches and coleslaw, Mr Schumacher arranges four yellow legal pads and four number two pencils around the kitchen table. He says this is how it's done in a law office. We take our places, and he instructs each of us to write down any suggestions we might have for the business.

At the top of a clean sheet of paper, I write:

KATE'S SUGGESTIONS FOR MR SCHUMACHER'S
CHOCOLATE CHIP COOKIE BUSINESS
1. Name of business (Something catchy)
2. Who bakes? (I do)
3. Who cleans up? (Pinky)
4. Who will buy the cookies? (Everyone in New York)
5. How much money should we charge?
   (Fifty dollars a cookie!)

"This meeting is called to order." Mr Schumacher bangs his gavel (actually, it's a small hammer from the toolbox Nana keeps in the linen closet) on the wooden table.

"Thank you for attending," he begins formally, "and for wanting our business to get off to a good start. The first thing on today's agenda is to name our cookie venture. Suggestions, please!"

"How about the Chewy Chip Factory?" Pinky smiles hopefully.

Mr Schumacher carefully writes it down under the heading "Business Name".

"Mrs Stein?" he says.

"You won't laugh?"

187

"Only if it's hilarious," Mr Schumacher answers.

"What do you think of Max's Makeshift Cookie House?" she says slowly.

"I like it!" I exclaim.

"Me too," says Pinky.

Nana grins. Mr Schumacher bangs his gavel on the table for the second time. "Time to vote," he says. "I vote aye."

"Aye!" say Pinky and I in a single breath.

Mr Schumacher pounds the gavel one more time. "It is unanimous. Max's Makeshift Cookie House!"

Then we all get up and hug each other. What fun this is going to be – and democratic. Mr Schumacher sure knows how to include people in his affairs. Too bad we have to go to school tomorrow. I would love to be here when Mr Klein's supersnow-plough of a truck pulls up at the front of our building and unloads one hundred pounds of cookie ingredients. The neighbours will go crazy, trying to figure out what's going on.

"Next on the agenda," Mr Schumacher is saying, "we need to talk about an advertising policy."

"What's that?" asks Pinky.

"We have to let people know we're in business, right?" he answers.

Pinky puts her fist under her chin, then says, "We can advertise in the *New York Times!*"

"That's an excellent suggestion," Mr Schumacher assures her, "but I'm afraid we don't have the funds – not yet."

"Oh."

"The important thing," Nana adds, "is to advertise cheaply."

"We can put signs in the elevator," I suggest.

"Good!" Mr Schumacher prints "Elevator signs" on his pad.

"But we have to expand beyond this apartment building," Nana insists. "Mr Schumacher's cookies are so good the whole city should hear about them."

"Hip, hip, hurrah!" Pinky sings.

"I'll ask Pat Mandella – she's class president now – to pass

188

the word around in school," I say. And *I'll* pass the word in ballet class. Instead of Girl Scout cookies, we get to sell Mr Schumacher's!"

"We need a press release," Nana says thoughtfully, "to let people know what we're selling. I can write it, and Pinky, our resident artist, will draw a design – our logo." Nana smiles at my sister. "Also, you can be in charge of running them off at the photocopy centre on Broadway."

Our meeting lasts more than an hour. Somewhere around nine o'clock Pinky drops her head across folded arms, and two minutes later she is sound asleep, her breath coming in even, rhythmic patterns. That's when Mrs Schumacher adjourns the first official meeting of Max's Makeshift Cookie House.

"I don't know, Peter," I complain, wrapping the long woollen scarf around my neck. "Less than a month till the audition, and look at me – a basket case. My stomach is in knots and I can't eat. I can't fall asleep at night and I'm convinced by the way Ron's been picking on me that my dancing gets worse by the day."

"I've told you a million times," Peter answers. "He *isn't* picking on you. He's trying to *help* you – because he thinks you're good."

"But am I good enough?" I sigh.

"You're just getting nervous," Peter assures me.

"Of course I'm nervous! Aren't you?"

He shrugs. "Nope. I can't afford to be."

"But it's more than nerves," I continue. "I think these NBS auditions are beginning to make me a little sick."

"Too sick for a soda at Jake's?" he grins. Sometimes Peter makes me so angry. He jokes when I want to be serious. He treats the most important day of his life – March 16 – as if it were no more important than a trip to the neighbourhood soda fountain. How can he be so cool?

We walk down the two murky flights from the ballet school. The late-afternoon sun makes long cold shadows on Broadway. Saturday shoppers whoosh by, carrying colourful shopping bags, pushing baby strollers, and mostly looking as if they needed to start the weekend all over again.

Jake's is a run-down but homey little candy store near the corner of Eighty-eighth Street. It is squished in between a gourmet treat centre and a fancy-looking health food store. Jake himself must be a hundred years old, and the story goes that he refused to sell his store for a million dollars, even though the rest of the block is being renovated into a glamorous shopping plaza.

A narrow and cluttered aisle leads to the back. We sit on two of the three wobbly stools.

"Yeah?" The teenager behind the counter looks as if he wouldn't know a bottle of shampoo if one fell on him.

"Orange juice, please."

"Root beer and a rare hamburger," says Peter.

I put an elbow on the counter and rest my head on my hand. "You see," I say slowly, "it's finally beginning to dawn on me that I'm never going to be a star."

"How do you know?" Peter turns the bottle of ketchup upside-down and barricades it with little cubes of sugar.

"I *know*. Sometimes you just feel these things. My grandmother always tells me I push myself too much," I continue, "and I think she's right."

"Yeah, but she never told you to *quit*." Peter flicks two

fingers against the side of the bottle and spins it around and around.

"It wouldn't be quitting. I am not a quitter."

He turns to face me. "Then why won't you audition?"

"I thought you were my friend, Peter." I shake my head. "You act as if you wouldn't talk to me again if I decided not to audition."

"I *am* your friend," he insists. "That's why I think you should audition. You'll never get anywhere if you don't go through with this."

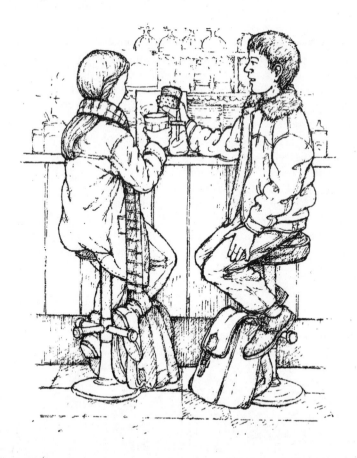

"So what," I mumble, thinking what a disaster it would be if Peter and that rat Ariane went on to the National Ballet School without me. Why, I'd be nowhere. Nowhere! Peter would be too busy and too proud to bother with a flunky named Kate, and the two of them would dance off, never looking back, never feeling the tiniest little bit sorry for me.

"Are you sure you want to be a dancer?" Peter is beginning to sound slightly disgusted with me.

I blow the paper off the straw the greasy kid put in front of me. I wish I could think of something brilliant to say.

"I don't know what you're so afraid of," he tells me, and his voice is kinder.

"The way I see it," I begin, "the difference between you and me, and between creepy Ariane and me, is that the two of you are willing to give up *everything* to dance."

Peter takes a long strawful of root beer. He stares ahead, at the ancient grill that sizzles his hamburger and the opaque plastic cups piled in the sink. Right this minute he looks much older, like someone too wise and sophisticated to be associating with a kid like me.

"Well?" I say. "Aren't I right?"

He smiles slightly, as if he'd just awakened from a pleasant dream. "It's my life," he says simply.

Peter douses his hamburger with extras. Extra pickles from the tinny bowl on the counter, extra onions, and about a pound of ketchup. He carefully cuts it in half. Then, like the

gentleman I always knew he was, he hands me my share. One thing about Peter Robinson is he always knows the right thing to do.

MAX'S MAKESHIFT COOKIE HOUSE
370 Riverside Drive
Manhattan

Max Schumacher's old-world recipe
for chocolate chip cookies can't be beat.
Try one and you will never go back
to the packaged variety. Expensive?
They may cost a little more, but
taste one and you'll see why. We use
the best ingredients money can buy.

Place your order today.
You'll wish you placed it yesterday.

We put one of Nana's press releases under each door in our building. I take a batch to school and hand them out at lunchtime. Pinky does too, and she brings a bunch to her music school in the Village. I volunteer to circulate flyers on Broadway, but Nana and Mr Schumacher veto that suggestion on the grounds that girls who stand on street corners have a knack for finding trouble.

Mr Schumacher's wholesale delivery came right on schedule. When I got home from school that Monday, bulky brown sacks of flour were stacked against the kitchen door. Blocks of butter were crammed every which way in the refrigerator, and bags of sugar, boxes of eggs, and assorted packages were stuffed into the tiled area under the old porcelain sink.

"Where are we going to put everything?" I exclaimed.

Nana was sitting at the kitchen table. She cracked one egg after another into a big glass bowl. "It won't be so bad," she answered. "We just need to get organized."

Mr Schumacher's sleeves were rolled up over his elbows. He used a long wooden spoon to blend cookie batter in a brand-new, extra-large aluminium pot. "And there's another feature to this business, Kate," he said, pointing to his left bicep. "I'm getting muscles at the ripe old age of seventy-one!"

"Muscles build character." I stuck my forefinger into the batter, smacked my lips loudly. "Delicious!"

"Kate." Nana pointed to the kitchen door. "Out, out, out!"

"Just testing," I called from the hallway, "like they do in the Betty Crocker kitchens."

That was just three weeks ago.

It looks as though Peter was right because the cookie business is really taking off. Mr Schumacher just may be a businessman, after all! Of course, now the apartment is cluttered and chaotic all the time. If the phone isn't ringing, then it's the doorbell. Orders. Reorders. Orders. More reorders.

If Nana and Mr Schumacher aren't stirring and mixing and counting out cookies, they're hunched over their long sheets of paperwork. Cold suppers have become routine; that is just as well since the taste of chocolate chip cookies seems to be in everything we eat. And even though Nana and Mr Schumacher keep talking about getting organized, I'm beginning to doubt they ever will.

"If this activity continues, we will have to open our own bakery, with a warehouse!" Mr Schumacher beams.

"Nonsense," says Nana. "We're doing very nicely right here. Besides," she adds, "the girls couldn't contribute as much if we were working downtown somewhere."

The truth is I love helping out with Max's Makeshift Cookie House. My main job is to hand out the press releases and tell people about the cookies. Publicity, Mr Schumacher calls it. But I am also allowed to take phone orders and sometimes I pack cookies for a pick-up. Mr Schumacher and Nana are the bakers, and Pinky delivers to customers in our building. Business must be pretty good because Mr Schumacher even bought a pocket calculator to make the arithmetic easier.

The funny thing is when I'm helping with the cookies, I actually forget to think about ballet. But then, when I least expect it, pop! The picture leaps into my head. I am that famous ballerina, beautiful and rich. I perform in the sophisticated cities of the world, but especially in New York where Nana and the others can come and see me. Me! Dancing every single day, dancing . . .

"You'll never get anywhere if you don't go through with this audition." That's what Peter said.

And nasty old Ron isn't being too subtle these days either. "You missed two Thursday classes," he said accusingly.

"I was baking . . . cookies . . ." I apologized meekly, but he walked away, and for the rest of class he never once stopped by to correct me. "Dance must be your *life*," he had told us that snowy afternoon.

195

If only I were a little kid again. Then Nana could tell me what to do. It's a curious thing with her. For the unimportant stuff ("Comb your hair!" or "Be home before dark."), she is so tough. But when it comes to the really big issues, like the NBS audition, my grandmother has the most annoying way of letting me make my own decisions.

"Nana!" I have been stalling for an hour. The French text is open, untouched, to the chapter on *pluperfect*. Lounging across my bed, I reach for the door and call to her. "Nana!" I repeat. "Can you come here?"

"I'm busy," she replies.

Swell. Too busy with Mr Schumacher to talk to her own granddaughter. I fall backwards and raise my legs toward the ceiling. Scissor kicks . . . one and two. Maybe Peter is right; if I would just audition, my decision would be made for me. If the judges select me, I'll go on to the National Ballet School this summer. If they don't pick me, well . . .

The door opens and Nana comes in brushing a powdery layer of flour off her hands and on to her apron. "What's up?" She sits on the edge of my bed.

"I thought you were busy." There I go again, saying things that sound so awful the second they're out of my mouth.

"Never too busy to talk with you." Her tone is sarcastic but she smiles and I am forgiven.

"I'm in a fix, Nana."

"What kind of fix?" she asks.

"I can't decide what to do about that audition." I tell her. "I'm just not sure I'm good enough."

"You're afraid you'll be turned down." She says it as if she were some kind of mind reader.

"That's part of it," I sigh. "The other part is I'm not even sure I *want* to study at the National Ballet School. Everybody says it's horribly competitive. They say the pressure is so great that kids are always having nervous breakdowns . . ."

"Kate," she frowns, "wherever did you hear such a ridiculous story?"

I shrug. "Just around."

"But you love your classes," she reminds me.

"I know, but I have a feeling it's kid stuff compared to the National Ballet School."

She nods.

"Peter says," and I stare down at the red plaid quilt on my bed, "maybe I don't want to be a dancer."

Nana makes a little clicking sound with her tongue. "One day you want something, and the next day you don't," she says slowly. "Grown-ups have that problem, too."

"Peter says I'd be a quitter."

"Nonsense!" She looks at me sternly. "Peter's whole life is ballet. He has made a total commitment, and nothing will stand in his way." Nana leans towards me and our faces are very close. "When he auditions on the sixteenth, it's because that's the right thing for *him* to do."

"I'm not a quitter, Nana."

"I know that," she smiles. Using her fingers like a comb, she pushes the hair away from her forehead. The soft white fluff reminds me of the flour from our cookies and the snow before New Yorkers traipse all over it. "And there's something else," she continues. "You may not be ready to audition right now, but it's important to remember you're only twelve years old – not exactly over the hill, even for a ballerina. Peter is a little older, and so is that Ariane girl you keep talking about."

"And what happens when the two of them make the NBS? What happens to *me*, Nana?" I mumble.

Nana takes a deep breath, then lets the air out slowly. "You mean, what happens when the two of them start going places and you're left behind."

I nod.

"It would be hard to take, all right, but you would learn to accept it," she says, very matter-of-fact. "That's no reason for you to audition, Kate."

"You don't understand," I sigh, but I know she does, and she knows it.

"One thing I've learned from all the literature you bring me on being a professional dancer is you don't *have* to study at

197

the National Ballet School at the age of twelve." Nana pauses briefly. "The point is, Kate, all won't be lost if you wait a year or two."

"Wait a year or two . . ." I repeat the words and suddenly they make sense. "Nana," I say softly, "maybe that's the answer – and I never even thought of it. I never even thought about next year."

When she hugs me it feels safe and good, like when I was little. When life was simple. "Sometimes we're so close to a situation that we can't see it clearly," she tells me.

"How will I know if I'm ready next year, Nana?"

"Suppose we take it one year at a time," she says. "It's easier that way."

"So much can happen in a year," I add. "Like with Mr Schumacher. Who would have thought, even half a year ago, that he'd be living here with us?"

"Certainly not I," she answers thoughtfully.

"Nana," I say, "are you having a good time out there with Mr Schumacher?"

"I'm having a very nice time."

"Sometimes I wonder if Mr Schumacher likes me," I tell her.

"Of course he does," she answers quickly. "He happens to be crazy about the two of you – you and Pinky."

"It's just that he's got so many important things on his mind, and maybe he thinks I'm in the way around here."

"In the way!" she exclaims. "There's no such thing as being in the way with your own family."

"I guess I'm still getting used to having an extra person around," I confess. "Probably, I wasn't so nice to him in the beginning."

"It does take getting used to," she agrees. She cups her hand under my chin. "What really counts, though, isn't how many we are, but how we *feel* about each other. Do you understand, Kate?"

"Yes." And then; "Do you think Mr Schumacher feels like he's a part of our family, Nana?"

"If he's smart, he does." Now she smiles.

I'm supposed to be sleeping like a log. When a girl makes a big decision, like the one I've made tonight, she's supposed to drop into a deep, sweet slumber. Not me. I squirm around for endless hours, trying to block out thoughts of the National Ballet School, of Peter and Ariane, of *pirouettes* and *fouetté* turns.

I visit with Nana quietly in the kitchen when it is midnight and then when it is one o'clock in the morning. We don't talk about ballet. In fact, we don't talk much at all. She makes me warm milk, which I hate, but she's right. It settles my stomach, and finally, I sleep.

I dream that I call on Mr and Mrs Stuffed Shirt Robinson.

"You may not remember me," I tell them, "but I'm Peter's best friend. Kate's the name. We plan to be married, but not yet. I came here to tell you a thing or two about your son."

"Oh, dear!" squeaks Mrs Robinson.

"Peter happens to be a wonderful person!" (I shout that part.) "He's kind and sensitive, and he kissed me. He helped Mr Schumacher get started in business, and he says the nicest things to my grandmother to make her feel good. Also, Peter is the best student at the New York Ballet Academy. He's going to be a star one day, you'll see!"

Naturally they are stunned. Such raves about their only son!

"Bring the finest wineglasses," Mrs Robinson orders her housekeeper, and the three of us toast Peter. Then that handsome boy comes in from the cold. He hugs me and kisses the tip of my ear. Wow! His parents start to cry and they apologize for not understanding how much dancing means to him. Then I wake up.

"Mr Robinson is a creep," I announce at breakfast.

"Kate!"

"It happens to be true," I say, carefully spreading a thin layer of butter on my rye toast. "He won't accept the fact that Peter wants to be a dancer."

"Perhaps," Mr Schumacher suggests, "he fears Peter's life as a dancer would be too unstable, unpredictable."

"Max!" my grandmother scolds. "The future is always unpredictable." She turns to me. "Knowing Peter, I assume he will audition over his father's objections."

"Yup," I answer and suddenly I feel very proud of Peter, proud to be his friend. "I wish his parents were supportive like you, Nana."

She pours herself, then Mr Schumacher, a second cup of coffee. I notice she isn't using her crinkly aluminium coffee pot, but the shiny electric one Mr Schumacher moved down from 14A. "Thanks for the compliment," she says.

Then Mr Schumacher turns to me and says, "What about you, Kate? Have you made up your mind about the audition?"

I focus my eyes on a small patch of green-flowered wallpaper directly in front of me. "Well," I begin casually, "it looks as if I've decided not to audition."

"That's not fair!" Pinky screeches. "Now I don't get to have a famous sister."

Nana looks at me. "Are you sure?" she asks.

"I think so." I watch the funny way the flowers twist and turn and whirl around each other. "Are you all very disappointed in me?"

"Disappointed!" repeats Mr Schumacher. "I should say not. It often takes a lot of guts to do what you feel is right."

"And it sure feels right," I sigh.

I bite off a small piece of toast, and another. I eat until there's nothing left, and then I reach for seconds. So, it's that easy. All you have to do is say it, and already you feel better. It doesn't even hurt. *I am not going to audition, and I'm going to live. I am not a quitter, and I still love ballet. I will take class for the rest of my life because I love the way it makes me feel.*

Now there is only one little problem to solve. I need to find a way to tell Peter. I need to make him understand.

PAULINE LEARNS A LESSON

NOEL STREATFEILD

from Ballet Shoes

*Adopted as babies by Great Uncle Matthew (otherwise known as Gum),
Pauline, Petrova and Posy Fossil live with his great-niece Sylvia, Nana
her old nurse, and several boarders – including Dr Jakes and Mr
Simpson. Now Pauline has been called for an audition; to buy a new
dress for it, each of the Fossil girls has had to sell a dearly-loved
necklace to Mr Simpson.*

THERE IS NO DOUBT a new dress is a help under all circumstances. This new one was very becoming to Pauline, whose hair had got no darker as she grew older, but had remained a natural platinum. All the children considered velvet the right material for an audition frock, and in Harrods, Nana and Pauline found a black chiffon velvet dress. It was plainly made, with a white collar and white cuffs, and a tight bodice with rows of buttons down the back. Pauline wished it was not black, which she thought dull, and like their elocution overalls; but it was the right sort of thing to wear, and had the advantage that there was an enormous hem to let down, and that the black knickers that belonged to her overall would do to wear under it. Mr Simpson waited outside Harrods in the car, and though it was too cold to take her coat off, Pauline unbuttoned it so that he could see what the money he had lent had bought. He said she looked magnificent, and all the way to the Academy he pretended he was driving a debutante to a Court at Buckingham Palace.

Pauline left her hat in the cloakroom, and she and Nana went and stood in the hall. Nana carried her coat, for the students were always inspected before they went to an audition. There was one other child waiting, who had her mother with her. Her name was Winifred and she was very clever. She acted really well, she was a brilliant dancer, she had an unusually good singing voice, but she was not pretty. She had a clever, interesting face, and long, but rather colourless, brown hair. She was wearing an ugly brown velvet frock; not a good choice of colour, as it made her look the same all over. When Winifred's mother saw Nana, she gave her Winifred's coat and shoe bag and hair-ribbon, and asked her to be so kind as to look after her, as she could not well spare a morning, as she had her husband ill, and there were five children younger than Winifred at home.

Winifred looked enviously at Pauline.

"What a lovely frock! I can hardly breathe in mine, it's so tight. I bought it last year out of the money I made in Pantomime. I've grown since."

Pauline flushed. It was not her secret how she had got the money for the dress, so she could not explain; but she did not want Winifred to think she often had things like that.

"I borrowed the money for mine," she whispered. "But don't tell the others."

Winifred nodded to show she would not.

"We're going for *Alice*, she said.

"*In Wonderland*?" asked Pauline. "How do you know?"

Winifred held out the hair-ribbon which she was holding.

"Whenever they put on *Alice In Wonderland* and they are taking people down about *Alice*, they tell them to bring hair-ribbons. I should think you might get it. I wish I would, though."

"It would be lovely!" Pauline's eyes shone at the thought.

"Fancy meeting all the people, the Frog Footman, and the Mad Hatter, and . . ."

"And think of the money!" Winifred added.

Pauline thought of the necklaces.

"Would one earn much?"

Winifred looked wise.

"It's the Princess Theatre; it's a mean management. Ought to get six, but it'll be more likely four . . . they might squeeze five."

"Five what?" asked Pauline. "Shillings?"

Winifred stared at her.

"Shillings! Pounds. Don't you need money at home?"

Pauline thought of Gum, and Sylvia's grey hairs, and the boarders.

"Of course."

Winifred pulled up her socks.

"There's needing money, and needing money," she said wisely. "If I could get this job, Mother'd put half away for me, but even what's left would mean the extra stuff Dad needs to get well. He's had an operation, and doesn't seem to get right after it. Then there's clothes wanted for all of us, especially shoes. Oh, it would be wonderful if I could get it!"

She looked so anxious that Pauline almost hoped she would. Of course she needed the money too, but somehow, although there was not any for new clothes, and the food was getting plainer and plainer, nobody had ever said what a help it would be when she could earn some, and certainly she had never worried about it as poor Winifred seemed to do. All the time Winifred was talking people who walked by called out, "Good luck, Winifred, good luck, Pauline." Pauline could see from the way they looked at her that they thought she looked nice, and from the way they looked at Winifred, that they thought she did not. She wished she had some money and could buy Winifred a new frock; she was so nice and she looked so all-wrong.

When Miss Jay came, she turned both Winifred and Pauline round and said, "Very nice," and though it was impossible that she thought Winifred looked nice in her mustardy-brown frock, which was too small for her, there was nothing in her voice to show it. She told them both that they were going to the Princess Theatre to be tried for the part of *Alice*, in *Alice in Wonderland*, and she asked for their hair-ribbons, explaining to Nana that it helped if they looked like Alice. She tied Winifred's brown ribbon first, and then Nana gave her Pauline's black velvet that they had bought in Harrods to match her frock. Miss Jay took a comb and swept Pauline's hair off her face, and tied it back, then she laughed and said she looked ridiculously Tenniel. Pauline was just going to ask her what Tenniel was, when she remembered he was the artist who had done the first *Alice in Wonderland* pictures. Doctor Jakes had told her so.

They drove to the stage door of the theatre, and went on to the stage, which was crowded with people. Eight were girls with their hair tied just like Winifred's and Pauline's, so it was obvious they wanted to be *Alice* too, and there were a troupe of children in practice-dress and ballet shoes, and a lot of grown-up people. Miss Jay asked Nana to comb the two children's hair, and she told them to change into their ballet-shoes and to take off their coats; she herself disappeared through the iron pass-door which separated the stalls from the stage.

Pauline tried to see where she was, but there was such a glare from the footlights that it was impossible to see more than the front row of the stalls, and that was empty. Suddenly a voice called out of the blackness of the theatre, "Is Mr Marlow there?" A man stepped out from the crowd on the stage, and came down to the footlights. He held up his hand to shield his eyes from the glare, and talked with somebody the children could not see across the orchestra well. The conversation was all about whether his voice would, or would not, do for the Mock Turtle. In the end he said he thought they had better hear him, and he came to the back of the stage close to Pauline, fetched a piece of music, and gave it to a man sitting on the stool in front of the piano. Pauline supposed he would sing some grand dull song, and was very surprised when he sang *The First Friend* out of the *Just So* book. After he had sung he disappeared through the pass-door just as Miss Jay had done, and for a long time nothing happened at all. The children in the practice-dresses limbered up, and did a few exercises on their points, which Winifred and Pauline decided they did very badly, and the grown-up people smoked; then once more a voice called out from the theatre.

This time it said, "Will all the children whose names I call out step forward, please?" Winifred's and Pauline's names were called, and so were all the other girls with their hair done like *Alice's*. They looked at each other to see what they ought to do, and then came down-stage and stood in a row in front of the footlights. They seemed to be there an enormous time while people whispered, and then a different voice said, "Little Fair Girl in black, what's your name?" Pauline was just looking to see if anyone else was wearing black as well as herself when Miss Jay replied, "That is Pauline Fossil". There was a lot more whispering, and then the other children were told to sit down. Pauline felt awful standing by herself being stared at by all the people on the stage, and all those she could not see in the stalls. She would have liked to have wriggled, and stood on one leg, but the Academy training had taught her not to stand just how she felt, so she stood as she did before a class, with her toes turned out, her heels together, and her hands clasped behind her back. After what felt like an hour, and was really only a few minutes, Miss Jay came in front of the stalls were Pauline could see her. She leant across the orchestra well.

"They are going to try you. Will you sing first, or do your speech?"

Every boy or girl at the Academy, when they were nearing their twelfth birthday, got what was called "m'audition" prepared. They meant really, "my audition", but somehow habit had turned it into one word. "M'audition" was a speech from a play, or a recitation, and a song which had a dance

worked to the chorus, or to a repeat of the tune. If a child was being seen for an acting part, or simply as a dancer, of course he or she only acted or danced, but every child had a full "m'audition" ready. Pauline had Puck's speech from *A Midsummer Night's Dream*, and a song called *Springtime is Fairy Time*, which had a waltz tune, and so was easy to dance to. She thought a moment, faced with "m'audition" for the first time, and then said she would do Puck's speech, for she knew it would be easier to act than to sing, when her voice was wobbly with fright.

The moment she started she stopped feeling frightened. She

had worked at the speech for hours with Doctor Jakes; together they had discussed exactly how Puck felt, and how he looked, until just saying the words made her feel that she had turned into a queer little creature who did not belong to the mortal world. When she had finished, Miss Jay called out that she was to ask her nurse for her music. Pauline turned very red, for she felt all the other children were thinking how much too old she was to have a nurse; she wanted to explain to them that Nana was not really a nurse, and anyhow Posy was still young enough to need somebody to look after her. But of course she could not, so she fetched her music feeling shamed. Although she had seen the Mock Turtle person give his music to the man at the piano, she did not quite like to do that with hers, so she looked at him first to see if he seemed to be waiting for it. He made things easy; he held out his hand and said cheerfully, "Throw it over." He seemed to know exactly what she was going to do, because he turned to the last page, and played a bit and asked her if it was the right time for her dance. Pauline did some little bits of the steps and said it was, then she went to the middle of the stage and sang.

She was very glad when she got to the end of the second verse, which was all the singing there was, for she had not a very big voice, and it sounded to her, in that large theatre, like a mouse speaking. She did not mind the dance so much though it was on her points, for there was not much of it, but it felt funny dancing in a velvet frock. The dance finished in a pose on the floor, and when it was over, Pauline got up, feeling rather a fool and wondering what to do next. A set dance like that if done at a charity performance ended in applause, and if done at the Academy ended in criticism; but no dance Pauline had ever seen ended in silence. She looked desperately round to see if any face showed what she ought to be doing, and there was Winifred making tremendous signals at the chair next to her. Thankfully Pauline ran to it, and sat.

"Was I all right?" she whispered.

"The acting was," said Winifred. "You were out of tune in

the song, though, and your ankle shook awfully in the *arabesque*."

Pauline made a face.

"I knew it did. I couldn't hold it; I got my posture wrong. I didn't know I sang out of tune. Was it very bad?"

"No, only to me, because I know the song."

Miss Jay's voice called out for Winifred, and she got up in an awful flutter, almost snatching her music from Nana.

"Hold your thumbs for me," she gasped at Pauline. "I did for you."

All the children at the Academy believed that holding your thumbs brought luck. The Fossils did not really, because everybody at Cromwell Road, except Cook and Clara, thought it silly; but they had to hold them if anybody asked them to, so Pauline gripped hers. But Winifred did not seem to need any help; she recited *You are Old, Father William*, and then sang *Come unto these yellow sands*, and then did a most difficult dance. Pauline released her thumbs, and looked at Nana, who shook her head. Neither of them said anything, but they both felt sure that Winifred would get *Alice*. Winifred herself did not seem a bit sure when she sat down; she said that being able to do things well did not mean you got on best, and that looks and personality were more important. Miss Jay came back through the iron door, and told them they had finished, and she was taking them home. She said nothing as they went up the stairs to the stage door; but when they were in the taxi she said gently to Winifred that she thought she would be engaged as understudy; they were going to try the other children, but she thought it would be all right. Then she smiled at Pauline.

"They are engaging you as *Alice*, Pauline. It's a wonderful chance."

Pauline was so surprised that she could only gasp, but Nana said:

"But Winifred did the better."

Miss Jay nodded.

"Winifred is the best all-round student the Academy has

ever had, but Pauline looks right for *Alice*."

Suddenly Winifred put her head in her hands and burst into tears.

"She looks right for everything, she always will. Oh, I did so want to get *Alice*! We do need the money so dreadfully."

Everybody tried to comfort her, but they could not, because there was the fact that Pauline was engaged for the part, and she was not. Pauline stopped being pleased, and felt miserable; she thought of Winifred's father, and her five brothers and sisters, and even being able to buy back the necklaces stopped being important.

Before Sylvia could sign a contract for Pauline she had to have a licence for her from the London County Council, permitting her to appear on the stage. The first step to acquiring a licence for children is to get their birth certificate, which is a quite simple thing to do; but Pauline had no ordinary birth certificate, for, of course, she had not got it on her when Gum found her floating on a lifebuoy, and since nobody knew whose baby she was, they had not been able to get it for her. Fortunately, Gum was a man who believed in things belonging to him being kept in order, and a baby without a birth certificate was not a baby in good order, so he had rectified matters by going to Somerset House, and having her entered as an adopted child. After that she had a birthday, and her birth could be properly certified. It was a mercy he had; for without proof that she was twelve, she could not have been granted a licence.

Sylvia obtained from the Education Officer's department of the County Hall a copy of the London County Council's rules for children employed in the entertainment industries. They were all good, and framed to look after the employed child's health and well-being. She filled in the application for a licence, and sent it down to the Princess Theatre, and somebody for the Princess Theatre signed those bits that concerned them. A week later, Sylvia got a letter telling her to bring Pauline to the County Hall on the following Wednesday, with her certificate of birth, both to be examined by the medical officer and interviewed by somebody in the Education Department.

Various people were nervous over this letter. There could be no doubt that Pauline was in the most bounding health, and rather ahead of her age from an educational point of view; but Doctor Jakes and Doctor Smith fussed inside themselves in case she should not be up to the required standard, and miss playing *Alice* through their faults. Nana knew that Pauline ate well, and slept well, and had as well-behaved an inside as any inside could be; but she was haunted by thoughts of the medical officer of health saying: "Who has had charge of this child? She has been very badly looked after." Sylvia could not eat for fear the representative of the Education Office should look at her with scorn as one trying to make money out of an adopted child. On the day of the interview, Nana cleaned Pauline's reefer coat, and blue beret, and laid out her newly washed jumper and some well-mended gloves, and when she was dressed said with a sigh, "You may not look smart; but you do look neat."

Mr Simpson drove Sylvia and Pauline to the County Hall. He tried very hard to cheer them up, but they were both silent with fright. They did not feel any better when they got to Westminster Bridge and saw the County Hall ahead of them. Really, going into it looked very like going into Buckingham Palace, it was so large and magnificent. Mr Simpson did not care a bit how grand it looked; he swept in at the front entrance, passed the policeman, and stopped his car right against the flight of stone steps leading into the main door.

"Do you think," Sylvia asked in a trembling voice, "that we ought to have come to this door?"

Mr Simpson gave a proud look at the door, and said that in a way it was his, it belonged to the ratepayers, and he was one of them. This made Pauline feel a bit better, and she was not as crushed as she might have been by the enormous hall surrounded by commissionaires that they walked into. The commissionaire they spoke to, however, proved to be a friendly man; he looked at Sylvia's letter, and he seemed to

211

know at once where she ought to be, and sent them to the lift. The liftman was as nice as the commissionaire, and took a lot of trouble to get them to the right room; but in spite of all this niceness both Sylvia and Pauline wished they need not knock on the door.

All their fuss was for nothing. The medical officer was just like their own doctor, and after examining Pauline, he laughed and said if he looked at her for a year he did not think he would find anything wrong. Pauline was a bit insulted by this, and told him that she had had measles once, and influenza twice. He laughed more than ever at that, and told Sylvia that he wished all mothers could produce as good a specimen as her ward. The Education representative was just as nice. He was very interested, when shown Pauline's certificate of birth, in her story, and so Pauline told him about Posy and Petrova, and he said he would be looking forward to meeting them when their time came for licences. He asked Pauline questions about her work, and she told him about Doctor Jakes and Doctor Smith. He read the letter they had sent, and then said she was a most highly educated person, which was a good thing for somebody who was going to play *Alice in Wonderland*, whom he had always thought a most well-informed child; what other child, he asked, who fell through a rabbit-hole would remember that she was likely to end up in New Zealand or Australia? He asked Sylvia what arrangements were being made for Pauline to go to and from the theatre, and she explained that though there would be a matron in the theatre, she could not let Pauline be alone, and that Nana was going with her to every performance, unless she went herself. The only part of the interview Pauline did not like was the part concerned with money. As *Alice* she was to earn four pounds a week, just as Winifred had said she would. The rule of the County Council was that at least one third of a child's earnings must be banked each week in the child's name in the post office, and the post-office book must be shown to prove that that much had been banked, before another licence could be granted, which, as a licence only

lasted three months, was a safe way of seeing it was done.

Pauline, who had read the rules, had worked out that twenty-six shillings and eightpence would go into the post office each week. Eight shillings a week would go to the Academy, who got ten per cent of her earnings for five years because they had trained her for nothing. That left two pounds five shillings and fourpence a week for Sylvia, and for paying back the necklace money. Pauline had decided that Sylvia ought to have thirty shillings a week to help with the house, and that would leave fifteen shillings and fourpence for the necklaces, which would buy back Posy's and Petrova's and pay six shillings and eightpence towards her own, which was very good indeed. But when the County Council gentleman asked Sylvia about Pauline's bank account, Sylvia said that she would always bank two pounds, perhaps more. Pauline gasped.

"Two pounds, Garnie! Why? You only need to put in twenty-six shillings and eightpence."

Sylvia laughed, and so did the London County Council gentleman, who said her arithmetic was admirable.

"But, darling," Sylvia pointed out, "I want you to have a nice lot of money saved by the time you are grown-up."

Pauline did not know what to answer, not being able to

explain about the necklaces, so all the time Sylvia and the London County Council man were talking about lessons during rehearsals, and after the Christmas holidays had finished, she was doing sums in her brain. Two pounds a week in the post office, eight shillings for the Academy, and thirty shillings for Garnie would only leave two shillings for the necklaces. It was most worrying, she could not get home quick enough to discuss matters with the other two and Nana.

Nana disapproved of getting into a fuss before you need.

"There's no need to get into such a state, Pauline," she said firmly when she heard the story. "To begin with, you don't know that Miss Brown will take thirty shillings a week, and second there's a way round every corner if you look for it. Now you leave things to me."

That night, after the children were in bed, Nana drew a chair up to the nursery table and took a pencil and paper, and did a sum. It took her over an hour, because she was bad at sums, but in the end it was finished, and she took the result down to Sylvia. She knocked on the drawing-room door. Sylvia was very pleased to see her, and told her to sit down. Nana smoothed her apron.

"Pauline will be earning four pounds a week in this *Alice in Wonderland*."

Sylvia nodded.

"I'm saving half of it for her, and I thought with the rest, which is one pound twelve shillings, for eight go to the Academy, we would get her some clothes."

Nana shook her head.

"That's all wrong, if you'll excuse me speaking plain, Miss Brown; and it's not fair on Pauline . Those children look forward to being able to help with their keep while the Professor's away." She sniffed to show what she thought of Gum. "Pauline will want a pound to go to the housekeeping."

Sylvia turned red.

"Nana, I couldn't. I'm managing. The money the boarders pay just keeps us and pays Cook and Clara, and you won't take any money . . ."

"Time enough to pay me when the Professor's back."

It was two years since Nana had let Sylvia give her any wages. "But because you can just manage, that's no reason to hurt Pauline's feelings. She wants to help. Now, what's right is" – Nana looked at her sum – "one pound for you for the house. Ten shillings for clothes, and two shillings a week pocket money for the children. One shilling for Pauline, because it's her earnings, and sixpence each for the others. It's over a year now since you were able to give them anything for themselves." Nana got up. "That ten shillings a week can be paid to me, because there's a bit owing on a dress that I got Pauline for her audition, and it's up to me to see it's paid back. Good-night, Miss."

Nana went happily to bed, and so did Sylvia who slept well for the first time for weeks; for there was no doubt Pauline's pound was needed, however hard she pretended it was not.

Pauline was a great success as *Alice*. All the papers said so, and published photographs of her. The children who came to see the play wrote her letters and sent her chocolates, and told her she was wonderful, and the grown-ups in the cast were nice to her, and she could not help seeing that they thought she was good. The result was she became very conceited. Petrova and Posy were the first to put up with it. Pauline thought because she was the leading lady in the theatre she was one in the house too, and of course they were not standing for that. It began with her telling them to fetch things for her, and to pick things up she had dropped. Posy, being good-natured, and not very noticing, did what she asked once or twice, then Petrova said, "Has something happened to your legs and arms?"

"Course not," Pauline answered. "Why?"

Petrova raised her eyebrows.

"I would have thought a person whose arms and legs were all right would have been able to fetch their own pocket handkerchief, and picked up their own wool."

Pauline flushed.

"Why shouldn't Posy? I get used to people doing things for me in the theatre."

Posy looked at Petrova, then they both looked at Pauline.

"It's going to be difficult," Petrova said thoughtfully, "when we are all working, isn't it, Posy?"

Posy nodded.

"All of us being like Queens at once."

Pauline got up.

"I think you're both being hateful." She slammed the door.

As the run of the play went on, Pauline got worse. She was very nice on the stage, because everybody was nice to her, but she was very different at home, and in her dressing-room. She had a dressing-room to herself; but it was arranged that Winifred should sit in it, because although there was an approved County Council matron in the theatre for the other children, they were all pupils from a different stage school, and Winifred did not know them, so Nana acted as matron for her as well as Pauline. Winifred's mother brought her to the theatre and fetched her home again, but Nana was responsible for her in the theatre.

As an understudy she was allowed to leave the theatre as soon as Pauline had gone on for the last act; but she had a dull job, especially for somebody as clever as she was, who could have played the part beautifully herself. It was difficult for her not to be jealous, with Pauline having all the fun, flowers, chocolates, letters, and praise; but she managed to pretend she did not mind, and spent all her afternoons knitting a jersey, and talking to Nana. Nana understood just how she must feel, and was very nice to her; but Pauline, getting more conceited every day, stopped being sorry for her, and bragged instead about what people had said, and all the presents she got, and even expected Winifred to fetch and carry for her. Nana was shocked that anybody she had brought up could behave so atrociously.

"Fetch what you want yourself, Pauline," she said. "Playing *Alice* hasn't lost you the use of your limbs."

"Oh, well, if Winifred won't help," Pauline grumbled, "but

I should have thought she'd have been glad to have something to do."

"Winifred and me have plenty to do," Nana retorted. "She has her jersey she's knitting, and I have enough to stitch with what you tear, so don't fuss yourself finding work for us."

Pauline messed about with her sticks of grease-paint.

"I shouldn't have thought there was much harm in asking a person to get something out of my coat pocket," she said nastily. "When I let that person sit in my dressing-room."

"If everybody had their rights," Nana answered quietly, "it would be you sitting in Winifred's dressing-room. Now get on with your make-up, and don't let me hear any more of that sort of talk."

Sylvia was very worried at the effect the theatre was having on Pauline, but Doctor Jakes comforted her. She said that the more puffed up Pauline became, the greater would be the flatness after the matinées were over, and that then she would learn that most important lesson for an actress – that today's success is easily nobody at all tomorrow.

"Let her learn," she said, "she'll soon find out."

After three weeks of being bumptious to everybody at home, and to Winifred, it became so natural to Pauline that she became bumptious on the stage. The rule of the theatre was that a cotton wrap had to be worn over all stage dresses until just before an entrance. Nana always saw that Pauline's wrap was round her when she went on to the side of the stage, and she hung it up for her when she made her entrance. When Pauline came off after the act, or during an act, she was supposed to wrap it round her. To start with Pauline was very good at remembering it, but after a bit she thought it a bore and left it hanging where Nana had left it, and the call-boy had to bring it to her dressing-room. This went on for a day or two; then one afternoon Pauline was skipping off after the first act, when the stage manager caught hold of her.

"What about your wrap, my dear?"

"Oh, bother!" said Pauline. "Tell the call-boy to bring it." And she ran to her room.

The stage manager took the wrap and followed her; he knocked on her door. Nana opened it.

"Good afternoon, Miss Gutheridge. Pauline must remember her wrap. The call-boy has other things to do than to run after her, and it is a rule of the management's that she wears it."

Nana called Pauline.

"Why did you leave your wrap on the stage?"

"Why shouldn't I?" Pauline said grandly. "Stupid things, anyway."

The stage manager looked at her in surprise, as up till then he had thought her a nice child.

"Stupid or not, you're to wear it."

He went back to the stage.

For two or three days Pauline wore her wrap; then one afternoon she deliberately left it on the stage after the last act. A few minutes later the call-boy knocked on her door.

"Mr Barnes's compliments, Miss Fossil, and will you go back for your wrap."

"Tell him 'No,'" Pauline shouted. "I'm busy."

"Pauline," Nana said, "go at once when the stage manager sends for you."

Winifred was still in the theatre, as Sylvia had invited her to high tea with the children after the matinée.

"Let me go." She jumped up.

"Sit down, Winifred." Nana's voice was quiet. "Either Pauline fetches it herself, or it hangs where it is."

"Let it hang, then." Pauline began to take off her make-up.

After a few minutes there was another knock on the door. This time it was Mr Barnes.

"Did Pauline get my message?" he asked Nana.

Pauline pushed Nana to one side and came out into the passage.

"I did, and I said I wouldn't fetch it, so please stop bothering."

Mr French, who was the managing director of the Princess Theatres Ltd, came out of the Mad Hatter's dressing-room, which was next door. He stopped in surprise.

"What's all the trouble?"

Mr Barnes looked worried, as he hated telling tales. But Nana thought a scolding would be the best thing in the world for Pauline. She told him the whole story. Mr French looked down at Pauline.

"Go and fetch your wrap at once. I don't make rules in my theatre for little girls to break."

Pauline was excited and angry, and she completely lost her temper. She behaved as she had never behaved before. She stamped her foot.

"Get it yourselves if you want it fetched."

There was a long pause, and in the silence Pauline began to feel frightened. Mr French was a terribly important man, and nobody was ever rude to him. His face expressed nothing, but she could feel he was angry. At last he looked at Mr Barnes.

"Is the understudy in the theatre?"

Nana called Winifred, who came out looking very nervous, for she had heard all that had gone on.

"You will play tomorrow," Mr French said to her, "Pauline will be in the theatre as your understudy."

He went down the passage and never gave Pauline another look.

Pauline finished taking off her make-up, and got dressed, and went home in perfect silence; her mouth was pressed together. Winifred thought it was because she was angry, but Nana knew it was not. She knew that Pauline was terrified to speak in case she should break down and cry. She certainly was not going to let the theatre see how much she cared, and of course she would not cry in the tube. As soon as she got into the house she raced up the stairs. She could not go into the bedroom, because the others might come in, so she went into the bathroom and locked the door, and lay down on the floor, just as she was, in a coat, gloves, and beret, and cried dreadfully. At first she cried because she thought she was being badly treated, and kept muttering, "It's a shame; I didn't do anything. Anyhow, Winifred's sure to be awful; they'll be sorry." But by degrees, as she got more and more tired from crying, other thoughts drifted through her mind. Had she been rude? Had she been showing off? Inside she knew that she had, and she was ashamed, and though she was quite alone she turned red.

Although Nana closed the nursery door, the other children could not help hearing Pauline's sobs from the bathroom. Nana had told Petrova and Posy something of what had happened, and although they knew that Pauline had got so proud that she would cheek anybody, they were terribly on her side now that she was down, and although they knew Winifred could not help being told to play *Alice*, they blamed her in a sort of way. Naturally, with all this, tea was not a very cheerful affair, and Winifred wished more than ever that she was not there, and still more that she could go as soon as she had finished eating; but she could not, as she had to wait for her mother to fetch her home. Directly tea was over, Nana sent them all down to Sylvia.

"Remember, now," she said, "Miss Brown hasn't heard what's happened, so none of you show her anything is wrong. You let Pauline tell her herself."

This made things much better. They played Rummy with Sylvia, and so that she should not suspect anything, were more cheerful than even they would have been ordinarily.

As soon as the other three had gone downstairs, Nana knocked on the bathroom door, and told Pauline to let her in. Pauline lay where she was for a few minutes, too tired and too miserable and too ashamed to come out; then she turned the key. Nana put her arm round her.

"Come along," she said, "you'll feel better after a bath and something to eat. When you are in your dressing-gown you can go down and tell Miss Brown all about it."

She treated Pauline just as if she were six instead of twelve, helping her off with her clothes, and even washing bits of her, then she put her in the armchair by the fire and gave her a large bowl of bread and milk.

"You eat all that, dear, and stop fretting. Pride has to come before a fall, and that's the law of nature; you've got your fall, and now you've got to be brave and get up again. What's one matinée, anyhow, and if you think right, you'll be glad in a way that poor Winifred gets a chance one afternoon. She's been very good, knitting quietly." Nana gave her a kiss. "I'm fetching the other two up, so when that bread and milk's gone you can have a chance to tell Miss Brown what's happened."

Naturally Sylvia had supposed something was wrong when Pauline had not come down with the others, and when she saw her swollen face, she knew it. Pauline sat on the firestool, and told exactly what had happened. It was a very truthful account. Sylvia heard her without a word, then, when she had finished, she thanked her for telling her, and said she was sorry, of course, but very glad for Winifred. This question of Winifred coming first from Nana, and then from Sylvia, made Pauline feel better; if she had to be punished, it was nice that it gave Winifred a chance.

At the matinée the next day she took a bit of sewing to do, and sat quietly in a corner working. She wished Winifred luck before she went on, and when she heard the Mad Hatter congratulating her in the passage outside, she managed to smile, and tell her she was glad, though inside she was not really, as of course she hoped nobody was as good as *Alice* as herself. Just as the last act started, Mr Barnes came to the door and called her. He was nice; he told her Mr French wanted to see her, and that though Winifred was very good, they'd all missed her, and would be glad to see her back tomorrow.

Mr French had a large office, where Pauline had never been before. He was sitting writing at a desk. He told Pauline to sit. Instead she came over to the desk and said politely that she was sorry she had been rude and disobedient yesterday, and that she would not be again. He said that was quite all right; she had done very nicely as *Alice*, and that doing nicely in a part always went to an actress's head to begin with. It was a good thing to get that sort of thing over at twelve, instead of waiting till she was grown-up. He then said that Winifred had done very nicely as *Alice* too, and that she might take note of it, because it was an object lesson she might remember always. That nobody was irreplaceable. Pauline looked puzzled, as she did not know the word, so he explained that it meant that you could always get somebody else to act any part – that the play was the thing. *Alice* was just as much *Alice*, whether Winifred was acting her or Pauline; Lewis Carroll's words were what mattered. Then he told her to run along; but just as she got to the door, he said that he was having a party of children guests round to see the play tomorrow, and she was not to hurry away, as he should bring them to call afterwards.

That night Pauline told Petrova and Posy about Mr French. Petrova said she thought it was true, and that though she did not think Winifred would be half as good as Pauline was as *Alice*, people who had not seen the play before probably thought her perfect. Posy said that she did not think it was a bit true.

"When I dance," she said, "nobody else will do instead of me; they'll come to see me, and if I'm not there, they'll just go home."

Pauline and Petrova snubbed her, of course, for though it was only a very Posyish way of talking, she could not be allowed to say things like that.

Pauline went to sleep feeling terribly glad the day was over and she would be *Alice* again tomorrow, and, down inside, rather surprised to find how right Mr French was. It really would not matter terribly if she was ill, and Winifred played for the rest of the run. She pushed the thought back, but she knew it was true.

Petrova went to sleep puzzling over what Posy had just said. She did not believe it was conceitedness when Posy said things like that, but it certainly was when Pauline said them. Why?

Posy went to sleep murmuring, *"Two chassés, pas de chat, pirouette, two chassés . . ."*

ACKNOWLEDGEMENTS

The publisher would like to thank the copyright holders for permission to reproduce the following copyright material:

Harriet Castor: Caroline Sheldon Literary Agency, London for *Grace*. Copyright © 1997 Harriet Castor.

Susan Clement Farrar: the author for *Samantha and Lizinka*, an extract from *Samantha on Stage*, Dial Press 1979. Copyright © 1979 Susan Clement Farrar.

Margot Fonteyn: David Higham Associates Ltd, for *Wartime Ballet*, an extract from *Margot Fonteyn*, her autobiography, W.H. Allen & Co. Ltd 1975. Copyright © 1975 Margot Fonteyn.

Jamila Gavin: David Higham Associates, London, for *And Olly Did Too* from *Prima Ballerina*, edited Miriam Hodgson, Methuen Children's Books 1992. Copyright © 1992 Jamila Gavin.

Rumer Godden: Macmillan Children's Books, London, for the extract *The Trouble With Salvatore* from *Listen to the Nightingale*, Pan Macmillan Children's Books 1992. Copyright © 1992 Rumer Godden.

Susan Hampshire: Reed Books, London, for the extract from *Lucy Jane and the Russian Ballet*, Methuen Children's Books 1993.
Copyright © 1993 Susan Hampshire.

Amy Hest: Amy Hest, New York, for the extract from *Maybe Next Year . . .* , Clarion Books, USA, 1982. Copyright © 1982 Amy Hest.

James David Landis: *Ugly Feet Are Beautiful*, an extract from *The Sisters Impossible* by James David Landis. Copyright © 1979 James David Landis. Reprinted by permission of Alfred A Knopf Inc, N.Y.

Michelle Magorian: Rogers, Coleridge & White Ltd, London, for *The Greatest*, first published in *You're Late Dad* edited by Tony Bradman, Methuen Children's Books 1989. Copyright © 1989 Michelle Magorian.

Jahnna N. Malcolm: HarperCollins Publishers Limited, London, for the extract *Rehearsal Revenge* from *Scrambled Legs: We Hate Ballet!*, Armada 1989.
Copyright © 1989 Jahnna Beecham and Malcolm Hillgartner.

Lynn Seymour with Paul Gardner: HarperCollins Publishers Limited, London for *Pulling Up The Old Socks*, an extract from *Lynn* – the autobiography of Lynn Seymour, Granada Publishing 1984.
Copyright © 1984 Lynn Seymour and Paul Gardner.

Jean Richardson: Penguin Books Ltd for *The Swan Mother* from *Stage Struck* edited by Jean Richardson, Hamish Hamilton 1991.
Copyright © 1991 Jean Richardson.

Noel Streatfeild: The Orion Publishing Group for *Pauline Learns a Lesson*, an extract from *Ballet Shoes*, Dent 1936. Copyright © 1936 Noel Streatfeild.

Jean Ure: Random House UK Ltd for an extract from *A Proper Little Nooryeff*, The Bodley Head 1982. Copyright © 1982 Jean Ure.

Cynthia Voigt: HarperCollinsPublishers for *Summer Camp* an extract from *Come a Stranger*, William Collins Sons & Co. Ltd 1987. Copyright © 1986 Cynthia Voigt.